KENTUCKY LOVE

KENTUCKY
LOVE

JOE COOMER

ST. MARTIN'S/MAREK
NEW YORK

Grateful acknowledgment is made for permission to
reprint from the following:

"The Waste Land" in *Collected Poems 1909–1962* by
T. S. Eliot, copyright 1936 by Harcourt Brace
Jovanovich, Inc.; copyright © 1963, 1964 by T. S.
Eliot. Reprinted by permission of the publisher.

"Voyages" from *The Complete Poems and Selected
Letters and Prose of Hart Crane,* edited by Brom
Weber, reprinted by permission of Liveright
Publishing Corporation. Copyright 1933, © 1958,
1966 by Liveright Publishing Corporation.

"Oh Pretty Woman" by Roy Orbison and Bill Dees.
Copyright © 1964, 1979 by Acuff, Rose Publications
Inc. All Rights Reserved. Used by permission of the
publisher. Made in U.S.A.

Design by Kingsley Parker

Library of Congress Cataloging in Publication Data

Coomer, Joe.
  Kentucky love.

    I. Title.
PS3553.0574K4 1985   813'.54   85-2662
ISBN 0-312-45161-X

First Edition

10 9 8 7 6 5 4 3 2 1

For Mark, Steve, Rusty,
Zeke, and Joe

1

I ALWAYS wake up remembering. Long before I notice the daylight or smell or hear or feel anything, even before I sense my own breathing, I am thinking about yesterday or last year. This morning I woke and was carried back four years, was still lying in the back of the hearse on its long slow cold January drive north to Decatur. We were on the Natchez Trace. It had been calm and simple that afternoon and evening, hundreds of miles of manicured wilderness, no traffic and no gas stations, not even a Stuckey's. But it was midnight now, the night full of itself, black and moonless. There weren't any signs or markings on the road, not even a center stripe, and no artificial lights of any kind. Bats dived at our headlights till Ford had to slow down; "I've killed a half dozen already," he said. Moto sat up front with Ford while I tried to get some sleep in back. I felt the pace of the hearse slacken, lying there, and so I rose up over the back of the seat, the green glow of the dash lights flashing off my teeth. I could see myself in the rearview mirror. Still the bats came at us, twirling out of the night.

They were starting to get to Ford. He'd been a wrestler in high school, but the bats had him pinned to the seat. "Either one of y'all want to drive?"

"Nope."

"Not me."

So he pulled over to the side of the road and we got out of the hearse to catch our breath. A fish splashed in the swamp down below us. We walked, stiff-legged, around to the front of the hearse and looked for bat damage, but there wasn't any: no blood, no onion-skin wings or brittle bones; just a single dull moth, his wings still beating faintly, risen from that warm swamp in January to die on the grille of our hearse. And then from Ford a little scream, high and night-rending, when a leaf fluttered down through the darkness, dived through the beam of a headlight and was swept up and out by the wind.

We laughed a little laugh, the three of us, and slumped back down into the hearse. Moto drove now, Ford took the back, and I sat up front and watched the road and made sure Moto didn't fall asleep. He drove awhile, and we opened up a couple of Big Reds and I said, "If a man does not keep pace with his companions, perhaps it is because he drinks a different soda."

And he said, "Yes," and, "hell, yes," and gunned the big hearse down along the long dark road; and he and I, we hardly flinched when the bats came at us again.

Then the memory is over, become memory of memory, and I am borne back to today. It is spring. I left the window open last night, the first time this year, and the sheer curtains have been pulled through to the outside and blow there, expanding and falling, expanding and falling. Maybe I opened it too early; I bring my hand up from under the quilts and touch my nose; it's cold. So I turn over and burrow a little deeper into the covers. The wind has gotten to the papers I left on the desk last night; they're scattered across the hardwood floor, and one is all the way out in the hall. They salute me with their corners when a breeze comes in. It is spring. The air through the window doesn't smell of anything, and the sky has nothing but its own blueness, as if the earth has lost its memory. And I am thinking about the blueness when I suddenly realize that I've missed the dawn again, slept through it, even with this east-facing window. I am going to have to work on that, stop staying up so late so I'll wake up earlier. I will have to catch it tomorrow. It is

2

supposed to be something different in the spring, billowing in over the knobs, and it's been a long time since I've seen it anyway.

I look over at the clock—seven fifty-nine—and I brace myself for the eight bells, not from this digital clock in my bedroom, but from Grandpa's old mantel-monster in the front room. It's this cyclops of a clock, mahogany case with sloping sides, that gongs these ball-grabbing gongs every chance it gets: on the hour, the half hour, quarter hour, and then some for fun because it's old. It must have been made for the blind or something. It shakes the whole house when it goes off, and it's taken me this whole year to be able to sleep with it. But it still unnerves me a bit in the morning. Almost any kind of clock noise bothers me; I'd always had a digital wristwatch till my dad gave me this special skin-diver holds-up-under-200-feet-of-water thing. I don't know why he gave it to me, it's not much use in the middle of Kentucky; I mean it never gets deeper than the bottom of my kitchen sink. But the thing about this watch is it ticks like a goddamn metronome, like somebody reminding you of something over and over. You just want to say, "All right! Okay!" Sometimes I will be listening to the ticking of that watch for half an hour before I realize that that's all I've really devoted myself to, the ticking of that watch. So anyway, I brace myself for the eight bells (a euphemism), pull up in a little ball under the quilts, and there it goes: GONG GONG GONG GONG GONG GONG GONG GONG. The house shudders, groans and pops, the wind blows harder for a moment, and it takes me three or four minutes to get warm again.

The morning seems to have remembered itself now. A sparrow flutters up to the windowsill and flutters off again, a car passes down the road, and I can hear Zeke pushing his plastic bowl around on the concrete side porch. He will be at my window in a minute or two, paws up on the sill, that great black snout sniffing, and then a whine from his empty belly. He is really the handsomest dog I have ever been acquainted with, miscegenation's better breed, a cross between Labrador and shepherd that left him black and big-boned, a smart mutt. He was Grandpa's dog, and now he's my dog—our dog, old black-snouted, crotch-sniffing, leg-humping generation-gapper.

He is here. He slaps his two oversized paws up on the sill (the middle toe on the left paw broken and pointed up, perpetually giving the world the bird), and lays his snout between them; the nostrils flare and collapse, flare and collapse, and then comes the whine. I sit up in bed, goose pimples immediately along my upper arms, and sniff my underarms—that old animal curiosity—to try and understand how he can be so sure I am here to listen to him whine. I take a chance that he is just guessing and slide back down under the covers, but the springs squeak a little, Zeke gets impatient and barks, perhaps his one bark of the day, and so I, my cover blown, toss it back away from me and sit up.

"Okay, okay," I say, and hear him thump back to the ground. And then, instead of the sound of his racing around the back of the house to the side porch to paw at the screen door, I hear a sharp rap and turn around to see him tottering on the sill, like the bird, all four huge paws pinned together in some exquisite canine ballet feat, till he crumples to the floor, victim of a misjudged transom. I get up and walk around the bed to him, my feet, like that witch's feet with the house on her chest, curling up, from the cold floor. I rub his wounded noggin, and he comes out of it fine, just a little batty-eyed. I pull the curtains back into the house and shut the window while Zeke takes two or three turns around my room. He pirouettes twice next to the cold gas heater and lies down to wait on me. I pull on the cold accordion of yesterday's jeans, let out an F-sharp when the zipper runs over my belly like an icicle, and think, I've got to wash clothes to-

4

day. A T-shirt ("Finite Man on Campus") and then an old sweater, some sweat socks and my sneakers, and I am ready to go.

I throw the quilts back over the bed and pick up the windblown papers, two of which have Zeke's earthy pawprint affixed, dogdom's notary seal, and I am a little proud of them. A subtle affirmation, much more important at the moment than the University of Kentucky diploma, with its gilded seal, on the wall above my desk. It's hung there for almost a year now, four years in the getting, and it's not that I'm not proud, it just seems the getting was much more promising than the having. If I could just apply this knowledge to a few other things I guess I would be a contented goddamn Plato or somebody, but there you are. Sometimes I could kick myself because I see things so clearly. I mean I never give myself much of a break. I tell myself I am hard to avoid, all alone in this big old house.

I guess, standing there at the desk, that it is going to be one of those days. I am going to follow myself all over the place.

A quick trip down the hall for a pee and a shudder, faint intimation of that last loss of heat, and Zeke and I go on to the kitchen. I am still young enough to feel that someone should be there already; it seems awfully empty. I flick the light switch, but it takes a couple seconds for the two round fluorescent tubes to take hold of all that electricity. I think it must frighten the hell out of them tubes. They throw a startled white light on the Frigidaire and stove and cabinets. The cabinets have been painted white at least a half-dozen times and they're hard to open. I pull a black cast-iron skillet out, the kind that will snap your wrist if you grab it off the stove full of gravy, and start frying eggs. Zeke likes his three fried, and eats them the way a human would raw oysters. I cook his first and set them aside to cool, then two for me and a piece of toast and milk. Such a domestic. American Gothic Break-

5

fast with Dog. I set the eggs, mine to eat and Zeke's to cool a bit more, on the table. The table is this chrome-legged Formica-topped thing from about 1947. I am told my grandmother, a woman I never met, gave her old oak table to Goodwill and brought this one in, yelling, "No more tablecloths, no more rings." I usually spend half of breakfast absentmindedly digging thirty-five years of crud from between the Formica and the chrome rim with my fork. Zeke whines from his belly and I fork an egg to him and he sniffs and I say, "See?" and yes, he agrees, still too hot, so I put it back on the plate. Impatient dog, but with a fine ability to reason and compromise. I look out the window and think this dog would make an excellent federal mediator.

The side porch and driveway are their characteristic blurred selves today. The window I look through is as old as the house, seventy-six, and the top of each pane is paper-thin while the bottom is a quarter inch thick. The glass is full of waves and bubbles; and like any stream it is ever so truly flowing to the sea. I feed Zeke one of his oysters. The rails of the side porch wave sinuously and the garage across the driveway leans dangerously to the left, a sunken barge amid a bed of kelp. The whole world is under water and I am saved by a trapped air bubble. Next to the garage, surrounded by stalks of dead sunflowers, the hearse stares blankly at me like a dead fish. I almost want to apologize.

But I am the one who is caught. This is usually the first part I think about, when I get started, the hearse. It was all such a long, long time ago and, of course, nothing can be done about it now. I have outlasted them all, really, in one way or another: the hearse, Ford, Moto, Grandpa, and even Mary, in one way or another, outlasted them all. I have really only had myself to contend with for the past three and a half years. And I really think now that I am doing all right. I am okay. It does not bother me anymore.

I spear Zeke his last two oysters and he swallows them and runs his tongue all the way around his head, the way you'd run a finger around the elastic waistband of your swimming trunks. He moves over next to the stove, does again two tight dog pirouettes, and lies down, screwing himself securely to the earth. Handsome as he is, he's a tired old dog, gearing down, while I am, just now, just now, beginning to get my courage up. I say, "C'mon," and he jumps up and follows me out the door into the yard, and, miraculously enough—we are really just amazed, gazing at each other with silly grins—we do not drown.

2

WE CHOSE the University of Kentucky, Moto and Ford and I did, because it was a long way from Fort Worth and because we could put my grandfather's Decatur address on our applications and pay the lower resident rate for tuition. Then we bought the thing, the hearse, two hundred bucks apiece, when we realized we had no reasonable way of getting back and forth. It really was a fine, fine car: a 455 under the hood, or the lid, as Moto (our ace mechanic) called it, and all kinds of starters and alternators and carburetors, all that stuff you need. You could stretch full out in the back if you wanted, of course, and get some sleep, which was a good thing: it's nine hundred and forty-seven miles from Fort Worth to Lexington and UK. It didn't smell bad or anything, if that's what you're thinking; we cleaned it all up and put a new tire on her. A '68 Cadillac, black with black curtains, but something had gone wrong with the paint job and it had this iridescent quality, like an oil slick on the street after it's rained. Moto built a little fake baby-casket ice cooler that we kept the Big Red in, which I admit was a little gruesome, and we always carried an old chauffeur's cap in case we wanted to get through a crowded intersection. No one questions a hearse's right-of-way, and the cops didn't stop us no matter how fast we went. Unwritten code, I guess. Respect for the hurriedly departing. Moto had this somber chauffeur expression that would just kill you. I mean if he pulled out in front of you at an intersection you'd been stuck at for half an hour you might get pissed, but then you would see his lower lip hanging down like a steak and you'd figure the guy had Romeo and Juliet in the back. I have always wondered if Juliet was pregnant when she died. Now there's tragedy for you. You see, I am chasing myself a bit there.

So anyway, it's about noon, and we are in the hearse four and a half years ago, January, pulling into the frozen gravel road to my grandfather's farm. The farm's about forty-five miles from UK, and I haven't seen Grandpa since the end of the fall semester, when Moto and Ford and I stopped in on the way home. We have to take the long driveway at a hearse's pace; the road up the hill is gouged with tractor ruts, and creekstone icebergs jut up out of the frozen mud.

"We are going to lose our muffler," Moto says. "We are all still virgins and we are going to lose our exhaust system." He says this in a very cold, just-to-let-you-know voice and it scares Ford a little bit. Ford had a car in high school that he couldn't keep a muffler on and you could hear him coming two miles off. He thought girls wouldn't have anything to do with him because of it.

"For God's sake, slow down, Hart," Ford says, and rubs his palms on his jeans.

I am driving. Hart is also my father's name. He was the

one named after Hart Crane, the poet, not me. I am named after my father.

So I drive along with my foot on the brake and Ford and Moto rest a little easier. We had had two priorities when we arrived at school the fall before: virginity and fraternity. We wanted to get rid of one and acquire the other. I know, you are thinking there is nothing new under the sun. But it is only you non-virgins who are thinking that. We pledged a fraternity, so we only had the virginity thing left, with three and a half years of college to go. We figured we were ahead of schedule. We figured we could even study awhile this semester. The pressure was off.

There were patches of snow in the shade of bushes and tree trunks, and on the right bank of the driveway. Grandpa raised hay in the summer to raise cattle in the winter. I could see him now halfway up the slope of the first "mountain" behind the house. The mountains were really only hills and knobs, but Grandpa refused to acknowledge that. He told everyone that he owned three hundred acres of mountains. He was on his tractor up there, pulling a wagonload of clover, stopping occasionally and shoving a bale or two to a herd of trailing whitefaced Herefords. He saw the hearse and waved, and I knew he would head down the hill soon, so when we finally reached the house we just went inside.

It was warm there, gas heaters in every room. Grandpa still had his little Christmas tree up, a spindly pine that might have been a branch off a larger tree. I fell in love with it. It was decorated with a gap-toothed string of popcorn and three red glass ornaments, survivors from my grandmother's time, hung with paper clips. The needles were beginning to turn brown and the floor beneath the tree was already littered with them. Moto brought in the baby-casket cooler on his shoulder and we went into the kitchen to look for something to eat. Moto and I pounced on a fresh box of Rice Krispies and Ford condescended

9

to an egg after I convinced him that the frying pan's lack of a Teflon coating could be overcome and that brown eggs were just as good as white ones. This was something I had over them. I'd visited Grandpa every summer for years and knew a little about farm life. I was on my second bowl of Rice Krispies when Moto took his first bite, satisfied, at last, that he had heard the dying fall and pop of the last Krispie in his spoon. Grandpa came in then, looking something like a grain of puffed rice himself, brown still this January and full of flesh and air. There were tears in his dark eyes from the cold and the veins in his nose were bright red. He rubbed his eyes and slid his hands across the white stubble of a beard and said, "Boys!"

There is something about a roomful of boys eating that tickled him to death. He started that grin which slipped into something like a gargle which erupted into laughter for no apparent reason and which always made me wonder what he had on life. He paused next to that sorry Christmas tree and pinched a kernel off and popped it into his mouth and began yelling, all at the same time.

I didn't hear a word. I suddenly realized that poor Christmas tree wouldn't come down till that string of popcorn was eaten. What would he do with those three red glass ornaments when all the needles had fallen off, the popcorn digested, and he had used that pitiful trunk for kindling? I always noticed things like this when I visited Grandpa, but always forgot them the moment I left his presence. Even though I was at the farm, for some reason or another, once or twice every couple of weeks during the next semester, I can't now remember when the Christmas tree was gone from its corner. I know that at some point a coatrack took its place, because it is there now, and was the following summer. I can't tell you how much this bothers me—that I don't know the exact moment he moved that damned lifeless pine out of the house. That moment is lost forever, and sometimes I feel it like the loss of the old guy himself.

He sat down across the Formica table from me with a rush of expelled air and sighing, slapping Moto on the neck and holding on, shaking him so that his back remained rigid while his head snapped back and forth. Moto had a spoonful of Rice Krispies in his mouth and I could hear the spoon clacking against his teeth. Grandpa finally let go of him with a "How you doing, boy?" and another slap on the neck.

"Fine, Mr. Scatter. I'm okay."

Then Grandpa, after folding his arms on the tabletop for maybe a whole second, looked across the table at Ford, and while Ford rushed to put his fork down and mumbled something about how fine he felt too, Grandpa reached over with both hands and boxed his ears. Then he folded his arms again on the table and leaned on them. The thing to do, of course, is to watch his eyes; I knew that, and I always knew that. But I got the brilliant notion that he wouldn't be able to do anything to me till the weight of his chest came off those wings he called arms. I got this notion just as he looped a boot around my ankle and drug me whole underneath the table.

"Good grief, Grandpa, I'm fine too," I said and he pushed his chair back and leaned down below the table's edge and sighed.

"You're a good boy, Hart. I've missed you, son. How was Christmas?"

"It was fine too, Grandpa. Momma's still mad at you for not coming."

I rubbed the back of my head where I'd hit it on the seat of my chair. Grandpa pulled himself back up to the table as I got up, that ceaseless smile across his face.

He said, "Well, I've got stuff to take care of. You can't just go to Texas and leave a hundred head of cattle with your best wishes."

"Impossible. Can't do it," Ford said.

"Out of the question. Ixnay," Moto followed.

You see these guys were real smart-asses with no respect for their elders, and they knew that when Grandpa had gotten you once he was fairly safe to be around. If you had told him you were fine or why not, he was as gentle as a pudding fart.

"Why don't you two puppy turds go find yourselves a closet apiece and play with yourselves," Grandpa said.

You see, Grandpa knew how to embarrass the hell out of two smart-ass freshmen with no respect for their elders. He said things like this to Moto and Ford all the time, and cursed with them, but never to or with me. I could be in the same room when he joked with them, fine, but he never looked at me. As though if he did my mom would somehow get wind of it. Ford and Moto were his friends, but I was his grandson, and you didn't make references to masturbation to your grandson. If Moto and Ford hadn't ever been around, me and Grandpa would have hardly known each other. But they were, a lot, and I think it brought me as close to him as almost anyone else had ever gotten. I was his grandson, and, by virtue of Ford and Moto, a friend he just didn't look at. He could love me and let me know he was human too. But it could be odd. He expected the same kind of behavior from me. Just before Christmas I came into the kitchen to sit down to dinner with him. Moto and Ford hadn't come in yet. As I was sitting in the chair I caught a fork sticking out over the end of the table and it flipped about six feet across the kitchen. I said, "Well, I'll be a son of a bitch," and he looked up and over at me from his hamburger as if he didn't even recognize me, as if I were the most disgusting potty-mouth that ever walked through his door. It was an awful look he gave me and I felt crummy for it all evening. If Ford and Moto had been there, it would have been nothing but funny and maybe there would have been a fork-flipping contest. He just had a specific set of behavioral rules for each of his relationships and I happened to get caught up in two sets. I just had to watch out.

As for now, Ford and Moto and Grandpa and I were

12

all together, and "turd" was an acceptable term. I poured the boys some Big Red to soothe their wounded psyches, and said, "There is nothing good or bad, but Big Red makes it so," and that brought them out of the dumps.

"You old sadist," Moto said to Grandpa.

"Bosh," Grandpa said, and got up and fixed Ford another egg and some bacon and poured out the last of the Rice Krispies in our bowls. Then he hurried us along with some story about a steer with an infected pus-ridden eyeball that was about to explode, which went marvelously with Rice Krispies. When Moto had coddled the last Krispie out of his bowl, Grandpa stood up and said, "Boys, what have you got planned for this afternoon?"

It was a pitiful sight: three grown boys sitting at a kitchen table trying to force some imagination through the aftertaste of eggs and Rice Krispies, knowing that if we came up with no plans we were in for an afternoon of hay or cows or barbed wire. It was simply too much for us. He had waited until there wasn't a Krispie to be spooned. The eighteen hours in the hearse had driven us to the state of mindless drudges.

I said, "Well, we have to be at the Fraternity House by nine tonight, Grandpa, but I guess we're free till then."

And so Moto went on and finished it out, did what had to be done, said, "What have you got in mind, Mr. Scatter?"

"Well," he says, "I don't want to take advantage of you boys, just off your drive and everything, but (but why not?) I've got a steer loose on the next farm and need to get him back. It'll take all four of us and Zeke to get him back through the same hole he tore open. Are you game?"

Tracked, shot, and stuffed. Oxen in human's clothing. Come nine hundred miles from Texas to herd a cow. I should have known, though. The only thing Grandpa liked more than boys eating was boys working. "There is nothing sadder than a boy with nothing to do," he would say. It would break his heart. He and I would drive into Decatur for a plate lunch at Spoonamore's on Saturdays; if he saw some guy sitting outside reading a *Playboy* or found a kid nursing a malt inside, he would make up an errand for them to run, some favor for him, an old man. I used to think he did it out of meanness, but I'm beginning to feel he honestly thought he was doing them a favor by giving them something to do. Moto and Ford and I weren't sad boys when we went to the farm on weekends. Grandpa was always doing us some kind of favor. This time it was cow herding.

"I can't tell you how much I would enjoy that," Ford said.

"Its emotional impact is beyond my communication capabilities also," Moto said.

I looked away from the window and said, "Do I hear cattle lowing or is that the mooing of my heart?"

Veritable pukes of laughter from us as we follow my deaf grandfather out the door. And we were off, Grandpa up on the tractor and me and the boys dragging our feet off the back of the wagon. Ford sang, "Green acres is the place for me . . ." but slowly, and with a somber tone, as if it were for a soap-opera love scene. Moto and I kick at frozen cow chips. The old tractor pulled us up past the pond and the tobacco barn, over two hills, and through a couple of gates. Then all three of us got the idea of rain or snow, the sky gray and damp-looking, and held our palms out. Nothing, but then we felt it again, rubbing our arms and the backs of our necks. Then Moto screamed, and opened his mouth the way Charlie Brown does when he's missed the football again. He pushed himself off the wagon and started slapping at his neck. He pointed, aghast, at Grandpa ahead of us on the tractor. And we turned, and about that time Grandpa leaned out over the fender of the tractor and spit out a long stream of brown tobacco juice that the wind whipped into long spiderweblike strands that rolled

14

and blew across the bridges of our noses, across our parted lips. You can't wipe your face long or hard enough after something like that. We rolled off the wagon too then, and walked alongside the tractor, just in front of Grandpa.

Zeke was waiting for us on top of the third hill, canine against the sky. He'd gone around the long way along the creek, looking for rabbits or whatever offered itself. Apparently he'd come up empty and satisfied himself with us. He met us at the crest and joined our ranks alongside Moto. It was like this. It was like two army columns merging in the desert. We all faced forward with stern expressions, marching along in the cover of the old Ford 8N, our heavy equipment, resolute in our determination to restore our borders, mend our fences: Grandpa the tobacco-chewing, grisly sergeant; Moto and Ford and I young but patriotic troops, and yes, afraid, but only a fool wouldn't be—we picked up rocks and threw them into the trees; and Zeke, faithful and brave ammunition dog, known to dash out upon the field of honor and drag home the wounded. Or we were knights and pilgrims on a search for the Holy Grail, a Sacred Cow.

We crossed over another hill, or mountain, I suppose, and through one more gate, across a field, and finally to the open section in the fence the cow had gotten through. Grandpa pulled the tractor and wagon over to the side and we all stepped through the gap in the fence. The field on the other side was small. The steer was in a far corner. He was fairly young, maybe only six hundred pounds or so, a wide-eyed white-faced stocky bastard that just looked at us. I didn't feel much like a crusader or soldier anymore. It was cold out; the wind was blowing off the hills, lifting up my eyelids, and big tears rolled out.

We started across the field, watching the steer, when it looked like a shiver passed through him, a glacier maybe,

15

and he bolted along the back fence, stopped, and bolted back.

"He's going to be a son of a bitch," Grandpa whispered, "he's going to be a son of a bitch."

Ford and Grandpa moved around on the left, Moto and I went to the right, and Zeke, who sensed that he had finally found something that wanted chasing, went straight up the middle. We humans reached the back fence and started moving toward the center, where the cow had stationed himself like a sawhorse, all four legs spread out and head lowered. He was aiming at Zeke. When we got within twenty feet of him on each side he bolted straight up between us, a beautifully executed draw, right at Zeke, our dauntless middle linebacker, who turned tail and ran in a long curving arc, steer on his butt, till Zeke broke left and right in quick succession and lost him. It simply amazes me how fast a dog can run with his tail tucked between his legs. We moved up behind the steer, forcing him toward the gap in the fence. It seemed easy. When he went left we compensated, throwing our hands in the air and yelling. It took Moto a couple of tries at yelling. He said he felt silly yelling "ho" at a cow like he was in a movie or something. But he did all right. It didn't look like the steer was going to stop once, headed straight for him, and he saw, Moto did, that "ho" was a useful and apt exclamation. It didn't embarrass him at all to say it. He said it a lot. He even said it a couple of times when he didn't really need to, when the cow was way over yonder.

We finally worked the steer up to the gap, and everybody closed in, yelling and waving arms and clapping. But the cow balked. He lifted his head and gazed over the other field, and finally balked. He turned, spun around, really, and met Zeke eye to eye, and Zeke cowered for a moment, but then worked out a halfhearted bark, and finally realized it was hopeless and started backing up. Then the cow shifted his gaze to Moto, who cowered a little too, but stammered out a "ho," which the steer ground into the earth with his front left hoof. Moto stepped aside then and the steer shot forward, but as he hit the gap in our ranks Ford locked himself, arms and legs, around the thing's neck. It was a great flying wrestler's leap and hold, I guess. The steer stopped and shook himself but Ford didn't let go. He had been riding him on the back but the shaking rolled him around till he and the steer were almost face to face.

Ford said, "Help."

Moto held his hands out the way you do when you don't want something hot thrown to you, and said, "Ho," and "ho."

"Don't let go of him, boy. We've got him now." And Grandpa did a quick circle around Ford and the steer. "Help him, boys. Get him, Hart."

Right. So I sort of rushed over and tentatively grabbed a back leg, and Moto got the other, and Grandpa took the poor thing by the ears and led him back through the gap in the fence, Ford still hanging on underneath. Back over, we all let go, Ford first, and the steer bolted off, to stop about twenty-five feet away and pick at a clump of grass, like nothing had happened since he was born. I loved him. We fixed the fence, and me and Zeke and Moto and Ford, who had cow slobber in his hair and ears, got back up on the wagon and Grandpa pulled us home, and he was so happy that he gave up his tobacco for us, and when it began to rain halfway back, we were sure and satisfied it was rain; we held our palms out and open, and watched the freezing water fall and roll in them, and we were very happy.

17

3

W E DO NOT DROWN, Zeke and I. We are corks, bobbing through the dew grass and over the creekstone in the driveway, latching on to the flotsam of the old wooden gate and finally beaching ourselves in the barnyard.

Zeke looks up at me and wags his tongue. He wants to know if I will let him jump for rats. I usually do, let him, though I'm trying to wean him because it couldn't be too good on his old body. I say, "Okay," and wave my hand toward the barn. He bounds across the loose dirt of the barnyard, does a dust-flying butt-rubbing slide to a halt at the barn door, and sits there calmly. Licks his paw. What about him?

We creep into the barn through the small door next to the big sliding one. It is still dark inside, still night inside; there are even a few stars above us: daylight popping through nail holes in the tin roof. Zeke slips over to the old corn crib along the wall, stops before the open door, and in the starlight I can dimly make out that he is pointing. Though he stares intently ahead, I know he is waiting for me to make my move. In the warmth, dark, and softness of the still barn we both listen to the rats. They are feeding on the dregs of a good year for corn. Grandpa filled the bin almost four years ago, but now there is only six inches of grain and mulch left. The rats have had time to gnaw through the wire mesh and now, every night, they come to eat what's left. I don't begrudge it to them, but Zeke does. All this is for his sake. I step quietly across the dry manure padding and unclasp the

18

hasp to the big door. Then a firm grip and I sling the door open: a huge grating noise and all the light in the world. Zeke leaps into the bin.

The rats scatter. And Zeke, intent on his purpose, does not bark, but scutters through the dry shucks from one end of the bin to the other, furrowing the grain with his lower jaw, hot on the haunches of one rat, then another, till they all escape him, squeezing through the holes in the wire mesh and climbing it, between the studs, to the ceiling. Zeke rears up on his back legs (and now he is as tall as I am) and swats at the rats as they climb with his unearthly paws. One of them drops back to the ground, but is still safe on the far side of the wire, and simply climbs back up. The ceiling of the bin is wire too, and the rats cross and recross it in their frenzy. This is where the jumping comes in. The bin is at least ten feet tall, and as powerful as Zeke is, there's no way he can reach the ceiling. But he jumps anyway, first crouching low in the corn, then springing up with all his might and will and snapping at those rats. He snaps, and falls sprawling in the corn, and gathers himself up and springs again and again and again and falls sprawling, until the rats are gone, and then he stands there staring at the rafters, his big pink tongue hanging down and dripping. He hops back out of the bin and looks at me. He is full of satisfaction, satiated with his own pure effort, his attempting. This is his rat meat, his dog bone. He moves over to me and puts his head underneath my hand.

And this is over and we go on with our business. Zeke goes outside to a water trough and I can hear him lap up three or four quarts as I walk to the far end of the barn and open the other big sliding door. The wind comes in then and goes on through, blows the dry straws and manure dust a few inches down the way. The old corn bin and a tack room are along one side of the barn and six stalls line the opposite wall. I stare the wind and the morning in the face for a moment and then turn with their pressure and go to Asia's stall.

Asia is expecting, not now, but soon. She is a very large horse, this Asia. She takes up all of her stall. She was not supposed to be expecting, but a very good stallion two farms over got loose one night last summer, and now Asia is expecting. He was an Appaloosa and perhaps the little foal will have spots all over his butt. Asia is plain brown, but the stallion had all kinds of spots, so the foal ought to have at least a half dozen spots. But who knows. In the meantime she is just very big and takes up all of her stall and I am taking care of her for a neighbor who's away.

She needs water, so I step inside, pat her on the neck, and pick up her bucket. She trembles a little, still not used to me, and watches closely as I step out and close the bottom half of the Dutch door. Outside, Zeke has found himself a cool spot. He is in the water trough, only his head above the waterline, hanging out over the end of the trough. "Get out of there," I say. "Are you crazy?" And he climbs out reluctantly, his tongue still hanging down about a foot. I dip Asia's bucket and give it to her, and then some grain out of a hundred-pound sack and into an old Revere Ware pot that's got no handle. This is what she has been waiting for, and she snorts a little when I set it down. I pat her brown neck again and close the door, and when Zeke and I leave she pokes her head out of her stall and looks after us.

We go just outside to the tractor port, which hangs on the barn like a fingernail that needs trimming. The tractor and wagon sit under it, in the shade, and we climb aboard. Zeke takes the wagon, hops up on its old oak bed, runs its length sniffing, and lies down. I sit on the black metal tractor seat that is shaped like the good hands of Allstate. Tractors have got to be one of the best things in the world. You sit way up off the ground in the open air and have all sorts of gears and levers and wheels and knobs to push and turn, and you can tow things, like the wagon, and push things, and tear up the ground and go up steep hills, and generally enjoy yourself in all sorts of manners. And everything is legal and part of hard work and I have never seen a bad guy on a tractor in any movie. So what I am trying to say here is I feel pretty good just getting up on this old tractor and sitting there.

We rumble out from underneath the shed and into the sun and then turn around and rumble back into the barn and shade. Asia sticks her head out of her stall again. I pull the tractor past her and just beyond the far door. The wagon sits directly under the open rectangle in the loft floor now. I climb the ladder and it is still dark upstairs, so I step over a few bales of hay and push out the loft door that opens over the barnyard. The house and most of the farm are framed in the doorway now, and every time I come up here and look out I want to find an artist somewhere and drag him back and say, "Would you just look at this?" and ask him if he could paint it right. I mean just get it right. It seems to me it would be an impossible thing to do.

I climb back over the hay and look down through the hole in the floor at Zeke on the wagon. He is still wet. He looks up at me and cocks his ears and leans his head one way, then another. He is completely baffled. I say, "Watch out," and drop the first bale onto the wagon. He finally gets the idea and dives under the wagon. The bales are heavy, but still bounce awkwardly as I drop them, and of the twenty we'll take out I have to restack six that have fallen off the wagon. Zeke comes out from under then and takes his place on the lead bale; I start up the tractor and we are off to feed the cows, my first herd.

We go up past the pond and through the first hay field and stop to open the gate into the second pasture. The cows aren't lined up along the fence the way they were all winter; the spring grass is enough to occupy them now. We go through the gate and stop again to close it, and

21

then down into the green pasture. The cows are here, sixty of them, white-faced heifers and a few steers. They look up as the tractor thumps toward them.

I don't know. It is so blue out. And the wind is blowing in the trees along the fence and down in the creek bottom, and these cattle move slowly toward us. This is so simple. I stop the tractor and listen to its last thump and watch the grass spring slowly back up where the wheels rolled over it. Zeke wags his tail as I throw off the first bale and break it open. He sniffs the bale and then lets the cows come in. And as I carry the bales out in a circle around the tractor and the wagon and Zeke and me, I am again and again and again overcome with a complete idleness of mind, a subtle satisfaction. And I think I realize, finally, what has been happening, what I've been doing for the past year on this farm: I have been jumping for rats; I have been putting my head under some huge scratching hand.

4

TRUTH IS, we enjoyed almost all the time we spent with Grandpa on the farm; broke off from school when we could, felt, I think, almost a sense of gratitude when we drove through the gate. But we hearsed out of the gate that evening, after the steer round-up, after Ford had forced a wet dishrag along each convolution of his slobber-brimming ear, after Grandpa had fed us again, hearsed out the gate toward what we thought was our certain destiny: consummations of joyous and, other than that, indescribable sorts. We turned out of the driveway toward UK and the Fraternity House and Ford brought us back full-circle to our purpose, said, "We didn't lose our muffler. We are going to do fine. I want a virgin." And we were all silent for a moment. The freezing rain had turned into gently falling snow. We were silent some more; we wiped our hands and mouths dry; if he had said, "Let us pray," we wouldn't have been more chaste in our actions. We were all hope and possibility.

My whole life is a book of days. By the time I'm seventy I'll probably only be a year long, a rainy day's read. Whole sequences, weeks and months, coalesce into the events of one compact day in my memory. In my remembrance I never have a free moment. January, February, the snow, school, Moto and Ford and me, that is all one day. I know this is not the way it was, but it is the way it is.

It started in the late evening. Ford and I were in the upstairs john of the Fraternity House brushing our teeth. It was eleven-thirty, bedtime. We were standing there in our underwear watching ourselves brush our teeth in the mirror when Moto burst through the door, plunged to the sink between me and Ford. He was in his underwear too, and he was crying. Big tears rolled down his cheeks. Then he screamed, "Don't look, don't look," and stood up on tiptoe, leaned over the sink, yanked down his drawers and flopped his old shang right out into the sink. "Don't look, don't look," he cursed at us, and started scrubbing at himself with both hands. The hot water blasted out of the faucet and steam rose up around us. Ford and I were foaming at the mouth. Moto bawled out something about jalapeños before bed, juice on his hands, and how all he had done was reach down to scratch himself, and now this. He was on fire. Ford and I went on brushing our teeth like nothing else was going on. Moto finished and limped toward the door. He said, "You guys didn't look, did ya?"

And so we would cleanse ourselves each night before bed. Ford and I walked back down the hall (visiting hours were over, so there wouldn't be any girls on the floor) to our room, and found Moto securely back in bed, his hands locked behind his head. Rank (he had a first name and there was more to his last, but we had forgotten the rest), our fourth man, was still up, though, listening to his "nobody touches the tuner but me" stereo and reading selections from his *Concordance to the Bible*. Ford and I climbed to our respective top bunks, his over Moto and mine over Rank, and then Ford stuck a long toe out and hit the light switch.

"Bedtime, Rank," he said.

And Rank, amid the bright halo of his desk lamp, gave forth his nightly religious sigh. He sighed for the whole planet. He marked his place in the *Concordance* with a piece of tassled silk and closed it reverently.

I said, "Where you at, Rank?"

And he looked up at me. "Tonight was Faith to Fall, Hart. I found some exciting listings."

"Gee, that's great," I said. I was merciless.

He said, "Yeah."

"Boy," I said.

Then I said it again, "Boy." I was despicable.

Rank got up out of his chair, opened his closet door, and changed into his pajamas behind it, so we wouldn't see. Then he closed the door and set himself up in front of his mirror and brushed his hair, reverently. It was a great black sea of hair that he brushed straight back over his skull, and divided in the middle in a deep wake. It was as if the Red Sea had parted. You almost expected to see a tiny Moses leading the children of Israel through his hair. He wet his finger with his tongue and pressed down a few hairs that hadn't found their level and, finally satisfied, he put his brush down. By morning the wake would be awash, Israel safe and sound, the Egyptians drowned.

Ford rolled over. "Turn off the goddamned light, Rank."

This was all ritual, so it didn't mean anything.

Rank plugged his earphones into the stereo and stretched the cord over to his bunk. Even with the volume down, I could hear "Bringing in the Sheaves" buzzing out of the headset. He folded back his quilt and sheet, turned out the lamp, and got into bed.

"Good night, fellas," he whispered.

Then he put his earphones on and we listened to his prayers. He thought that if he couldn't hear them, nobody else could. It's just like when you're a kid, playing hide-and-seek, and you think they won't see you, find you, if you can't see them, so you put your hands over your eyes. He prayed for the whole planet. He prayed for fifteen minutes.

He quit, and then somebody ran down the length of the hall with a raging chain saw, but then the house was quiet.

It must have been an hour, hour and a half later, that Rank took up with himself. I could hear a choral group of ants singing "Amazing Grace," and out in the parking lot two or three guys were yelling off beers. The bunk heaved and rolled with his rowing, and I lay there looking up at the dark ceiling, riding it out.

Moto woke Ford and me up for the second time next morning screaming and spitting. (Rank took a seven-fifteen class in calculus; his alarm let us know we had two more hours to sleep; he had to buy three alarms that semester.) I thought I had never gone to sleep. Moto was out in the middle of the floor wiping his mouth with somebody's jeans.

"What?" we said. "What is it?" And we sat up in our bunks.

"I was having," he slobbered, "I was having a dream about oral sex and I woke up."

"Yeah?" I said. "Too bad."

"Who?" Ford asked.

"Nobody," Moto spat, and rubbed his mouth again. "It

25

don't matter. I was having a beautiful dream about oral sex and I woke up with my face in my armpit."

Ford and I wiped our mouths with the length of our forearms.

"And my tongue is all sore," Moto whimpered.

Ford rolled out of his bunk and fell on Moto's, then rolled out of it onto the floor, like a barrel over the falls. He laughed so hard he had to hold himself in at the sides, but that just seemed to squeeze it harder out of his mouth. He had no compassion.

I said, "Man, I think I'd be brushing my teeth."

And he said, "Right. Right, Hart," grabbed his kit and was gone down the hall.

I stepped over Ford, picked up my towel and Moto's and headed to the showers. "I am holed up with a bunch of sex misfits," I said, more to myself than anyone else, but Ford heard and rolled himself out into the hallway, still holding his staves.

He said, "Be sure to let us know when you get it right, Mr. Professional Lover. Okay, huh? Let us in on it?" And he rolled himself back into the room. He was enough.

Steam billowed out of the bathroom when I opened the door. Moto had finished brushing and was now gargling furiously. I pitched him his towel. There were seven guys in the showers, and by the time Moto and I turned the water on, Ford was there too and the place was full, five nozzles on each wall and a body under each one. The steam rose up around us and puffed out the open window at the end of the room. The showers were on the second floor and fronted the street. The Fraternity House was between the sororities and the main campus. The window was always open, even in February, snow on the ground, icicles forming on the sill.

Ford took the nozzle nearest the window and brought our attention to Woman when she walked along the sidewalk. We didn't do anything if she walked by, it wasn't that, we just liked to know she was there, even if she did have six layers of clothes and a coat on. It was proximity. One of the guys might whistle sometime, but that was it. It was too damn cold to stick your ass out over that sill.

We acknowledged Woman a couple of times with a nod and hello and then started to settle down when Ford launched one of his pagan songs. It was "Pretty Woman." I thought there was another girl on the street but it was just the song. So he started in, you know:

> "Pretty woman, walking down the street.
> Pretty woman, kind I'd like to meet, . . ."

I joined in, and a couple of other guys then, and so all of us at once, singing high and low, wheezing and gargling, slapping walls and clapping our feet on the tiled floor. We rocked without our socks. Everyone sang along except Moto, who came in on the "mercy" and "okay," the tiger growl, "rowrr," that stood for base lust, which he could understand. In the meantime he choreographed. He said, "Like this," and snapped his fingers and pointed and spun for us, showing how, and pretty soon we had it, were all in the same motion, a pack of naked Pips. We smiled and spun in unison and moved a pointed finger around in a slow half-circle when we sang, ". . . walking down the street," put our thumbs on our chests for "kind I'd like to meet." We gathered at the window, and girls gaggled on the street and we wagged our fingers at them while we sang. "I don't believe you, you're not the truth, no one could look as good as yoooooo." They loved us. We loved them. And of course that brought the song into shore. But not before a flashbulb lit us up from behind and all ten of us said, "Hey," at once and colored. Whoever had taken it was gone with a guffaw, out the door and down the hall. Then the hot water played out and the girls drifted off and Christ, we were in school again.

"I'm gonna find that guy and kill 'im," Ford said.

We followed Moto back to the room after drying off. It

27

was a slow walk. He kept stopping, closing his eyes, snapping his fingers and saying, "Mercy." He was eat up with himself.

We dressed Moto in one of his twenty-or-so black T-shirts with a rock group on it, Ford in his tight white dress shirt and jeans that were three sizes too long so they crumpled up at his ankles—it looked like he crushed them with the breadth and weight of his chest. I put on the one sweater we owned between us, which was quickly fuzz-balling itself into nonexistence.

And we were off, with our notebooks, coats, and the Nerf football, for some breakfast at the Wildcat Grill. We had lunch and dinner at the Fraternity House but had to forage our breakfast on campus. Rank came in as we went out, finished with his classes for the day. How can you care for a guy like that?

We dropped off the curb on the corner of University and Hilltop and passed the Nerf the hundred yards or so to the Grill. Threw the ball between us almost all the way, to within ten feet of the door, when four girls came out and we found things to do like look at the sky, the snow, our watches, in a book, the other way, until we were upon them and we came out with a series of "hellos." One of the four looked our way. The rest were buried in their coats.

We got inside to a table and Moto said, "I think one of them girls was a fox."

"How do you know?"

"Law of averages."

I said, "Beauty is Big Red, Big Red beauty—that is all ye know on earth, and all ye need to know."

And we ate our eggs.

First class was Ancient History, not that we had missed it, but that's what it was, Ancient History. We talked about things like Diogenes, that old Thoreau, and the World of Iron, and Nineveh's Burden, and the Growth of the Church, Octavia, Antony and Cleopatra, the Fertile Crescent. All stuff we were vastly concerned with at the time.

28

Professor Ashurnasirpal, as we called him, Ashpal for short, was much more vivid. He had a glass eye that used to go dry on him, and as a professor of the chalkboard, drawing out genealogical relationships of ten thousand years of Assyrian kings, chalkdust would gather on his lower lid and burst out at us when he batted his eye. The effect was heightened with colored chalk. An enigmatic moment in history, and puff, a blue cloud of befuddlement would surround him. But he came in that morning completely without his eye, a black patch covering the hole and a brilliant white cast on his arm. He said, "I'm sorry, but I'll have to cancel class today. Don't worry about anything till next time. I'm truly sorry." And then he started to leave. His hair was bedraggled and his shirt wrinkled and he didn't have any socks on. He sniffed a little. He started to leave, and reached the door, but we were all still in our seats. And sometimes in your life, when you don't expect it and aren't ready for it, right in the middle of everything, you bump right into somebody. He stopped and said, "You know, sometimes the most loving thing in the world you can do for someone is leave them," and he went on out the door. We could hear him walking down the hall. The door swung to and fro until it stopped. It was the saddest thing on earth.

Moto said, "What about that."

And we said, "What about that." I think it scared us to death.

A girl up front whispered, "Poor old Ashpal," and the whole class drifted out of the room like it had been a wake.

Outside, Ford burped, "Bwoaaoarp," a long good healthy one considering our light breakfast.

Moto screwed up his face. "One of these days you're gonna do that and I'm gonna look over at you and see your intestines hanging out of your mouth."

"I'd just tuck 'em back in; it's happened before."

"Crimany."

Ford hit Moto in the back of the head with the football

and I caught the rebound, and we spread out along the sidewalk toward the Student Center tossing the Nerf. We passed around the frozen fountain and Patterson Office Tower, over old what's-his-name with his snow-capped noggin, along the front of Buell Armory with its ROTC cadets maneuvering around a basketball hoop inside, and finally a bolt down the walkway and into the Student Center.

Immediate composure: Domain of Woman. Fly check, finger comb, suppression of heavy breathing, periscope up: "Warning, warning, warning," Moto said in the robot's tongue, "a Fertile Crescent at seven o'clock." And true enough, she came rising out of the stairwell to our left, a bronzed blonde in February, which meant money enough and time for the trip to Florida and tan lines to boot. We followed her down the hall and through the aisles of the bookstore, lined up behind her at the snack bar, and hovered like flies around her table while she ate pizza.

"She has huge protuberances," Moto said.

"You think we're blind, Sherlock?" Ford coughed at him.

I said, "Go ask her out, Ford."

"Are you out of your mind? You go ask her out."

"I'm not gonna just walk up to her. You gotta have some kind of reason for just walking up to somebody like that."

"Why?"

"Well, she'll think you're trying to pick her up or something."

"You would be, you asshole."

Moto said, "There's no reason why you shouldn't be able to walk over there and just talk to her. Everybody is a human. Who else would she talk to?"

"That might be the one, for any of us," Ford said, "and here we are sitting on our dicks."

Moto said, "Boy, I wish I could sit on my dick."

30

"Okay," I said, "okay," and I took my wallet out.

"You gonna give her money?"

"Right, Moto. Keep your thinking cap on there, old pard."

I stood up, dropped my coat on the back of my chair, squeezed a few fuzzballs off our sweater, and didn't look up till I bumped into her table. I actually coughed to get her to look up at me.

"Excuse me," I said, "do you have change for a dollar?"

An expression of complete bafflement went over her face, like I'd asked her how many miles it was from here to the moon. Then she brightened. "No, but you can probably get some at the snack bar over there."

"Oh. Yeah. Thanks." So, with a pocketful of change, I walked over to the snack bar and stood in line again. I could hear Moto and Ford ripping themselves apart behind me. I stood there, and stood there and stood there. A slow line. Talk about wasting your life away for appearance's sake. Other people in the lounge were starting to notice Ford and Moto. They were beating the table when they could make a fist and pointing at me when they could hold their arms out straight. Anything was better than this. I ducked out of line and went straight back to the bronzed blonde's table and sat down.

"What I meant awallago when I asked if you had change was I was wondering if you might be if you could see your way through to going maybe on a movie out or something. Well?"

And she said, without pause or breath, "You're real cute and I appreciate the offer, really thanks, but aren't you sitting with that guy at this table behind me?"

And I said without pause or breath, "Yes, the guy in the white shirt? That's Ford, my roommate."

"No, no," she said, "the other one, the one with the black T-shirt on."

And I said, with a long pause and huge breath, "Why, that's Moto; why?"

31

And she said, "Well, would you mind asking him if he was in his Philosophy class yesterday? I wasn't there and I was wondering if he could come over tonight and help me out. Would you mind asking him?"

And I said, gasping, "I didn't know you were in that class. Ford and me are in that class too."

And she said, "Well, I'm not there often, but would you mind asking him?"

And I said, wheezing, pleading, "Please don't make me do this."

And she said, "Pleeeez?"

And I said, "All I wanted was change for a dollar."

A slug could've beat me back to our table.

"No luck, huh?" Ford asked.

"All kinds of it. None of it mine or yours, though. She wants to talk to you, Moto, you gob of phlegm."

"What'd I do?"

"She's in our Philosophy class. She wants your help with her homework tonight. She wants to talk to you."

"Right now?"

"Next semester."

"You aren't fooling me, are you, Hart?"

"I could just puke."

Moto got up and moved toward her as if she might suddenly take out a whip and flay him. Ford and I could barely stand it.

"It's true?" he asked.

I just nodded. Moto was sitting with her now, across the table. She was doing all the talking and he just nodded a couple of times and came back. Never said a word of his own.

"Well?"

"Well, I'm to go to her apartment tonight, with my notes, at ten-thirty."

"That's all?"

"She said she thinks she adores me. She isn't sure."

"Jesus, Mary, and the Alamo," I said.

32

"Why, though," Ford said, "there's got to be a reason. I mean, why." He didn't ask it. He just sort of stated it. The way you do when your dog dies.

"I don't know," Moto said. "Hart, I'm scared."

"He's scared," Ford said.

About that time she loomed up behind Moto, slid her hand across one of his skinny shoulders, and said, "See you," and smiled. Teeth like a row of alabaster Britannicas.

Moto said, "See ya, Virginia."

"Virginia?" Ford gasped.

"That's her name," Moto said. "I'll probably get cancer and die before ten-thirty."

We got up, and I put my dollar back in my pocket, and we struck out for Sociology at Memorial Hall. We didn't throw the football; we didn't talk.

When we finally reached the steps of the hall, Moto turned to us and said, "Well, I think I can handle myself," and then went on up the steps, two at a time, and inside. He was serious. Ford and I just looked at each other and then followed him, but it was as if we were running across a muddy field in slick boots. What was the use?

Inside, we found Moto and sat down, three among eight hundred, packed like saints into an old church to learn about the social behavior of man. It was more like crowd control. We all opened our texts to Chapter 6 at the same time and I swear the curtains on the left side of the auditorium billowed. The professor read the first sentence of the chapter (which wasn't my first sentence at all; it was inked in above the original first sentence: "This book sucks out the ass to say the least of the class." I had made social contact with some long-gone previous owner of my text) and eight hundred pens scratched it down; it sounded like a 747 touching down. At that particular moment the hall was relatively quiet. There were only fifty or sixty people coughing and maybe another twenty-five sneezing, and one girl in back who was a wheezer. Not to mention the background noise of seventy-five or eighty foot-tappers, a couple hundred pencil-drummers, and eight or ten compact-snappers. There was an argument going on up in the balcony, but you had to expect and accept a little flare-up now and then among eight hundred people. Statistics. It was our professor's great interest to interrupt the argument, bring the two or more arguers to the front of the hall (a five-minute walk from the balcony), and we would, as a class, discern the anthropological and sociological roots of their little spat. Perhaps it was a social more or custom facing change, a vague area in sexual roles. We would discuss, mediate, and resolve, and finally send the parties back to their seats, happier, more understanding human beings. Sometimes, one of the parties might say, in front of the whole hall, "Hey, now I understand where you're coming from."

The professor read from his book, our text, on the sex roles of Mbuti pygmies. I watched Moto. He shook his head in agreement at every sentence. I thought he might roll his eyes and holler "Amen" at any moment. Who was he now?

On the way back to the Frat House after class Moto said, "I think I'll be a sociologist." His eyes were still a little glazed.

Ford bipped him in the head with the football to bring him out of it and I caught the rebound. We walked three abreast over the icy sidewalks while Ford sang "Under the Boardwalk." Moto and I came in as background vocals. Ford would sing "Under the Boardwalk," and we would say, "With his baby," right behind him. People looked at us as we walked and sang but you couldn't look up at them or you'd lose the whole thing. So we walked all the way back to the House singing and studying the audacious existence of our very own toes.

Lunch was hot dogs and chili, which wasn't chili as we knew it, and so we passed. We dropped our books off in

34

the room. I headed for a few laps in the pool at Memorial Coliseum, Ford put on his shorts and sweats and set out for the weight room at Seaton Center, and Moto said he was going to get in some extra sleep. Always the optimist. Rank was already at his desk, through with all his classes for the day, his homework for the next month. He was just looking for a way to eat his meals and brush his teeth a few weeks in advance too. God's own eagle scout.

I took the hearse to the pool, not because it was a long walk there, but because it was a long walk back with wet hair. Lucked out and found two spaces together, tail to nose, in front of the Coliseum, and parked. After I'd gotten out of the car and dropped a coin in both meters I saw the lady who'd pulled alongside. She must have been behind me when I parked. She'd wanted one of my spaces. She shook her fist at me. I really felt awful but I acted like I didn't see her and ran into the Coliseum. I wasn't going to spend all afternoon searching for two more spaces when she could look for just a single.

The pool was almost empty, a guy practicing dives and two girls sitting side-by-side, dangling their feet in the water while they wrapped towels around their hair. I jumped feet-first in and dropped slowly down to the bottom. This was my home.

My favorite movie for years was *Mr. Limpet* with Don Knotts. He was this 4-F twit who wished he were a fish and became one, all form and grace and finally at home. He meets this lady fish and a crusty hermit crab and together they win the U-boat war for America in old WW Two. The girl is not a bad-looking fish either, and at movie's end they, the lady fish and Mr. Limpet, swim off together. It used to break me up, I was so happy for old Mr. Limpet.

I pushed off the bottom of the pool and rocketed back to the surface, breaching and rolling over into fanning butterflies down the length of the pool. I was at home. Grandpa had taught me how to swim when I was four, carrying me on his shoulders for a whole summer out into the big pond by the house, where I would climb down off him and then circle him with a frantic dog paddle. He was slippery but solid as a rock, and after a five- or six-yard swim I would come puffing back at him all elbows, heels, and knees and dig in. By the end of the summer I could swim all the way in to shore and then back out to him. All he would say was, "Good," and, "Swim over yonder now." And I would oblige. Ever since then I have been a loon for the water. I had my folks put a pool behind the house back home and bought a little john boat when I was fifteen so I could get out in the middle of a lake. A whole world of water. For now, this pool was the Hellespont, and Hero was twenty laps away, so I swam, back and forth, one stroke and then another, kicking off and then dragging my legs, turning around and kicking myself back across the pool, and then a lap under water. And finally I surfaced, winded, agog, but she was not there. So I climbed out and sat for a while, dripping, netting breath. I was still me, an ark, having to hold at that narrow horizontal of the surface, keeping my head above water, a gasp away from drowning and a drink from dehydration. I made my slow way back to the showers, as if I hadn't had enough water, changed, and drove home.

It was almost dinnertime and we were all going to a movie at the Student Center later on. *A Boy and His Dog,* or something. Well, I could handle that. Keep my head off Moto and the bronzed blonde. Ford got back from Seaton Center about the time I did. Moto was just waking up. He had worn a T-shirt to bed in case he had any oral sex dreams. Rank came in too, back from a blood drive or something. We cleaned up a bit, Rank parted the sea, and the four of us trundled downstairs when the dinner bell rang.

The living room was already packed with hungry boys. Grandpa would have been in heaven. Rank left us to con-

36

verse with the Housemom, and we hung out with Wyeth and his crew, four river rats from Cloverport, Kentucky, who made up the better part of our table, the back table, which lacked a degree of edicut. Second bell sounded and we jammed, forty of us, into the dining room. Moto sat down and Ford and I yanked him back up by the armpits again; he never remembered to remain standing while Mom did, till one of the forty of us prayed. The president asked Rank to "give us a prayer."

"Heavenly Father, bless this food we are about to consume, make our bodies strong to your music, which is above all else. Bless this brotherhood, Heavenly Father, help us see our shortcomings. In Christ's name we pray. Amen."

"That was nice, Ogden," Mom said. That was Rank's first name. Ogden.

Mom sat down finally, so the rest of us could.

Edicut prevailed at the back table. "Pass" was an unknown verb. "Reach" took its place in speech and action. Our goal was to eat, to gorge, down our food as quickly as possible, to carry all our plates and utensils into the kitchen, and fold up the table and stack it in the utility room before the other tables had poured their tea. We were of the philosophy that eating was a major waste of time at a university. It took us, max, eight, nine minutes to finish and wipe our hands on our jeans. We all gathered around Mom and the head table and asked if we could be excused.

"Please." She smiled. She despised us and loved us. We went back upstairs to get some studying out of the way in the same manner.

Moto said, "I forgot what we had for supper."

So I bipped him on the back of his head with the heel of my palm to break loose some of the mortar he called a brain. Maybe I was just getting one in for the bronzed blonde.

"Remember?" I asked.

"Oh yeah." And he smiled. At dinner, as I forked a piece of ham and dragged it back across the sky in front of Moto's face, he had taken a chomp out of it. It was a fair back-table practice, but you still hated it happening to you.

We slid into the books, knowing we had maybe thirty minutes before Rank finished dinner. He'd come up then and turn on his "Christian Country" AM station and the night would be done for studying. Ford took the time to switch the speaker plugs and turn the volume all the way up on the stereo. But that was beginning to be a nightly thing. Rank would come in and push the power button and about blast us all out of the room.

Ford would say, "Gosh, Rank, I must have hit the volume while I was folding clothes."

And Rank would say, "That's okay, Ford, I've done that myself sometimes."

While Ford and I went over a few calculus problems, Moto copied his Philosophy notes in a neater hand.

Ford said, "Don't give her those notes for a thank-you, Moto. You get something out of them, you hear?"

"I'll do my best," he said.

"Lord," Ford despaired.

Rank came in and all three of us had to go to the bathroom at once.

"Must have been all that tea we drank so fast," Moto explained as we stepped out in the hall.

We got fifteen or twenty feet away and heard the sound blast, waited till he turned the volume down, waited a little more, then wandered back into the room. We didn't know our own names.

Rank was piqued. He wouldn't talk to us at all. I felt awful for him, all of us ganging up on him like that, so I asked him to go to the show with us. I knew that would mean no ad-libbing the screen or slouching. Rank always acted as usher for the three rows in front and back of him. But he just put his headphones on. He was piqued to a *T*.

So we let him simmer and spent the next hour working on Moto: sent him down to the showers, ironed one of my shirts, got some cologne from Wyeth, and shined the rubber toes on his tennis shoes. We put two condoms and ten extra dollars in his wallet. When he came back from the showers, red and puckered from staying so long, we checked his nails and gave him his underwear that we'd washed. The pledges, fraternity initiates, had stolen every pair of underwear in the house during a meeting and we hadn't found a single pair yet. He dressed himself, put some hog hairs in his mouth and moved them around ritually, grated his face, did all those things Nacirema people do, according to Sociology class. Well. We were through. All that was left was his personality.

We moved out into the night.

"On Broadway," we rumored, mumbled, trolled through the dark alleys of campus, muffled in caps, coats, and scarves. No one would recognize us. A frozen mist boiled down past the sidewalk lamps and campus security drove slowly by us. Anything could happen this night. A bird, half-frozen, huddled against himself, chirped once from a low branch.

"Something's going on here," Moto whimpered and he turned all the way around.

"You're just nervous," Ford said.

All the same, we broke into a trot and beat it to the safety of the Student Center.

Total, maybe, ten people in the whole theater. But *A Boy and His Dog* wasn't bad. It's a future-world thing: The bomb has happened and everywhere is desert, and this boy and his dog, who's telepathic, wander around searching for food and women. We could relate. The plot thickens when he runs into this nude girl and she leads him to a netherworld where everybody is a Kansas wheat farmer. All the men are sterile, so they need this boy to impregnate all the women folk. Couldn't believe his luck. Only, instead of the women he gets a machine that sucks him dry every so often. But the girl who tricked him down there turns double agent and gets him out, but only after she pulls a few other underhanded double-crossing Communist-type incidents that almost get the boy killed. When they get back topside, the boy finds his dog has waited for him all this time. The poor dog is about dead from hunger, but so are the boy and the bitch girl. She suggests, I think, they leave the dog and get on with looking for some grub. But the boy realizes his old dog will die if they do that. So he kills the girl and feeds her to the dog. The credits roll as you hear the dog licking his chops. We cheered. The girl was a great loss, it was true; we all agreed she had quite a set of imponderables. We were not totally without morals when it came to women. We knew, in our heart of hearts, that a friend, an idea, was more important than simple sexual gratification. We just wanted to make sure how well we knew.

It was ten-fifteen when we came out of the show, so Ford and I sent Moto on his way with his notebook. Virginia's apartment was only a few blocks away.

"Good luck," we said.

And he said, "I'll miss you guys."

Ford and I walked home. There was nothing left for us to do. The moon dragged us back across campus as silently as any tide.

Rank was already in bed with his headphones, so Ford and I climbed up to our bunks as well. I tried to stay awake, but eleven rolled into twelve and twelve into one and I fell asleep. I suppose Ford did too. Waiting and worrying wouldn't help matters.

And then all I knew was all the light in the world was in my eyes and Rank was screaming. Moto had burst through the door, flipped the light switch, and tripped backward catching the cord to Rank's earphones, yanking them off his head. Rank was on the floor screaming and had his ears all bottled up with his palms. Moto was on the floor too, one leg propped up on a chair and the other under his butt. He was, apparently, deliriously happy. He smiled but didn't say a word. He was also freezing to death.

Rank stopped screaming long enough to point out that Moto was "stinking heathen drunk" and ask if he was bleeding, holding the side of his head up for our inspection. He wasn't, although both ears were already decidedly purple.

Ford and I jumped down.

"He's Key-Largoed," Ford said.

"He's afflicted," I said.

"I yam yot," Moto said.

"Hart, she got him drunk and stole his notes," Ford said.

"And his coat, too," I said.

Moto looked up at us and smiled again, and then he took on a wizened, puzzled grin. "Boys, did you know that womens has little black hairses on theys titties?"

"You goddamned liar," Ford whispered.

Rank stopped his moaning and moved closer.

"They do too," Moto affirmed.

"I've seen at least five hundred magazines," Ford whispered again, "a thousand girls, two thousand titties, and not one of 'em had a hair on it."

"They pull 'em out," Moto grinned, "with tweezers."

"Where are they?" I asked.

"Underneath, where they sag down?" Rank offered.

"Nope, right on the old bull's-eye," Moto answered.

"Bullshit," Ford said.

"How do you know?" I asked. "She just tell you all this?"

Moto wriggled up to standing. "First-hand, me boys. She don't think tweezers is natural."

"Really?"

"Really?"

"Really?"

He almost fell over. "I tweedle-deed and tweedle-dummed her rosebuds with my tongue."

41

"Goddamned liar," we said, as we carried him down the hall to the showers. We stripped him down to his shorts and stood him under the hot water. He didn't want to talk any longer. I think he suddenly realized he was cold. He slapped his ribs with both hands and said, "Where's my coat?" And we told him he came in without it. "It's at that Pancake & Egg Place. We gotta go get it. It's got my wallet in it." Ford and I remembered our condoms and money and dragged him out of the shower.

We were in the hearse and across campus in five minutes. It was four-thirty in the morning. The three of us blustered into the empty all-night café and Moto led us to his booth. The coat wasn't there. I went to the lady standing at the cash register and asked if she'd found a coat.

"No, I didn't, but I think Mary found one." And she hollered through the kitchen door, "Mary, bring that coat you found out here. This boy's come back for it." We stood around the cash register, patting our feet, trying not to inhale a pungent syrup-smothered egg odor. And then somebody backed out of the kitchen door with a pail of water and a coat. I looked at the coat and saw it was Moto's and breathed relief.

And then I looked at her. She was the morning and the moon and the sun. She was terrible. She was beautiful, and when I first saw her it seemed the air was purged, and then and there all my desires fell cruelly in after me and have ever since pursued me. I was changed. She handed Moto his coat and he found his wallet, everything intact. He thanked her and she said, "Sure." She didn't even smile. She drew me like water from a tap. There were freckles across the bridge of her nose and sprinkled on her cheeks, and when she gave Moto the coat the lamplight lit up the light-brown hair on the back of her neck. Before I knew it I was back in the hearse and driving. What had happened? At the house Ford and Moto were talking about the bronzed blonde again but I couldn't hear them. We climbed into bed and Ford toed

42

off the light and the whole world was undone. I fell asleep and dreamed, dreamed about catching the football, and got it all mixed up with the waitress who'd said, "Sure," and she threw me a long fast-fading pass and I turned running, running to get under its fall, and all I thought about as I ran was her utterly unfathomable beauty.

5

THE CATTLE school about me as I move slowly through them. I am looking for any sign of grass tetanus. In the early spring, bluegrass and fescue and clover gorge themselves on the rain, like they'd never heard of the stuff before, and subsequently the cattle can get too much water and not enough vitamins. They become lethargic and one day simply lie down and can't or won't get up. There's nothing you can say to them. I move among them and look for a drooping eyelid, a weak knee. But none of them seem pooped. They are all wide awake. And so I climb up on the wagon and turn to counting them, and get to twenty-one before I have to start over because Zeke has them stirring, changing places, cowering behind one another, falsifying identification papers.

"Desist," I scream at him. "Come here." And he looks up, gazes in three different directions, all of which I am not in, and then finally turns to me with his ears raised and squared off. "Get over here," I yell. And he hops over to me like I'm going to give him something to eat. I am exasperated. He has probably saved himself with that ploy a million times. The old "I've got the brains of a fish but the heart of a widdle wabbit" ploy. Your very oldest dog ploy in the book.

I count again, my hand firmly grasping Zeke's collar: and my kine are all at home. I have nothing to worry about. If I had a staff I'd live among them. If I had a pipe I would play. My dog is my only authentic piece of equipment. Although I sometimes think he would rather play the wolf.

"Let's go," I say, and rub his smooth head. We jump down off the wagon, leave the tractor and walk down the hill toward the creek. The cows don't even watch us go. Zeke runs ahead, as he always does, and I take it slow, as I usually do. I have all the time in the world and he is an old dog. His time has always been seven times more precious than mine. And so sometimes I will run with him and it is all he can do to keep from telling me I'm okay. But today I walk, and occasionally he will stop in his running and look back at me to make sure I'm following. He would rather not go alone.

"I'm coming," I yell, and he pivots and runs again.

We are going for our daily walk over the farm. It is the least we can do. And the most we can do. It is the best thing we do. I put my hands in my pockets and follow Zeke.

Beneath us, among other things, there is something like ten thousand feet of marine limestones and shales, two miles of it, a life-born series of rock that formed at the bottom of the sea. We are only a thousand feet above sea level now, practically on the beach, so I test each step for mushiness. Maybe I should carry a snorkel in my back pocket. We might have to swim for it at any moment. Perhaps like old John the carpenter I should keep a tub tied in the attic. Haven't they had to pull Plymouth Rock back up the beach? I stomp the ground in front of me a little more and look for clouds.

Zeke has almost reached the trees that line the creek.

44

He stops, hikes his leg in a crude arabesque, and immediately throws back his head and begins to howl at the sky. This is comic opera. But something is wrong. There is a natural grace to all of his actions, but now everything is wrong. He has an agonized expression, hunched shoulders, a dropped wrist, a caved-in elbow, and affected paws. I trot down to him and see why. His barre is an electric fence, a single wire I've stretched at about eighteen inches high and charged so the cows won't get in the creek. Zeke is peeing right on it and still crooning to the blue ether. He doesn't seem to be able to move, so I put the rubber sole of my sneaker on his flank and give him a shove. He falls over but jumps right back up. It didn't faze him one bit. Christ, maybe it felt good; maybe I ought to try it.

I step over the fence and Zeke clears it with a six-foot jump and we move slowly down the steep slope that bottoms out at creek. And the water is still running downhill; the ocean isn't yet on the rise. The creek is banked by a line of oaks and hickories on each side, escorting it to the sea, as if it wouldn't go there, that briny low spot on the earth, without a good shove in the bank. It is a narrow stream, spring-fed and clear unless we get a heavy rain, that serves as border to one side of the farm. It moves quickly, ice cold, through creekstone and over algae-slick shale and around black tree roots. We follow it down toward sea level, ducking behind tree trunks. There is plenty of light but the sky above us now is green, with only shards of blue appearing and disappearing as the wind blows. Perhaps the blue will fall down on us like leaves this fall. I toss a stick out in the middle of the stream and we follow it. It races, slows, pivots, submerges, and surfaces. It reaches a thirty-foot stretch of rapids and loses us, drops out of sight over a small fall, and by the time we get there it could be any one of two hundred sticks in a slow whirlpool at the foot of the fall. We look for a moment, then give it up, fall ourselves to looking

45

under rocks in the creekbed. I pick up one, lifting it by its slimy corner, and Zeke, pointing, sees him too: a big ol' crawdad, that creek domestic—cousin, I guess, to our scorpions back in Texas, which, they think, were the first critters to crawl out of the ocean onto dry land and make it work. They traded their flipper in on a stinger and crawled under another rock. Not much difference. Life goes on. You do what you gotta do. I give the crawdad a little nudge and he squirts out over the creekstone and disappears underneath another rock. That's why their kind has lasted so long: There's always been plenty of rocks to dive under. Maybe we should learn the trick.

Maybe we should learn the trick. Keep a few big rocks handy, within fifteen or twenty feet or so, of our nuclear-missile silos, prime targets, et cetera. One on every city street corner. One in every schoolyard. Economical too. Yes. Dive under them and peer out when it's all over: a bright pair of eyes in the dark cleft. Safe. It's an idea.

Zeke and I move along, among dogwood and oak, vines and trailers, to a more or less level spot, a quarter acre of bottom land that the creek moves only slowly through. The ground is cleared here. The creek has a grassy bank; it makes no noise. In the middle of the bottom, fed by the creek, is a perfectly round pond. It is an old sinkhole. When Grandpa was a young man, he and his father watched the hole suddenly collapse and take in the creek like a bottomless throat. The creek went completely underground and was seen no more. The ground drank and it drank and it drank. Farmers downstream, who'd suddenly lost all their water, came to look. The University sent people to look. They all stood on the rim of the hole and looked. They began to throw things into it. At first just rocks and any trash they found nearby, and later, whole truckloads of sand and cement. It all washed away down the hole while they watched. So they gave up. And three years later the hole closed in by itself. The water from the creek filled it in a couple of days and spilled over into the old dry creekbed and ran as strong and clear as ever. Leaves from the only tree in the bottom, a huge sycamore, sprinkled the new pond's surface, and the water reflected the branches of the big tree and the sky in between.

And this is what Zeke and I look upon, wander about, now. The grass is up to my thighs here, where the cows can't get to it, and I can just make out the waving tip of Zeke's tail as he moves through it, looking for rabbits. The pond, the scattered leaves, the mirrored surface, it is just an old impression for me, a vague recollection. This interruption, this marvel of a disappearing act that I can now see myself in, this tranquil beauty, is Mary. These floating leaves, brown from the fall before, are the freckles across her cheek and brow. I toss a stick into the pond and the blue sky breaks apart and falls down in shards upon me. I look around but there is no nearby rock big enough to dive under. I can think of no workable dog ploy. I yell at Zeke and we disappear into the trees on the other side of the clearing. It is an old pain that I have learned to handle, but sometimes things come upon you.

We go on, along the creekside, and I scratch Zeke when he wants it. Things come back to you; you're able to understand completely what years ago was the most baffling mystery. I come back to Ashpal, and that day in class about loving and leaving, letting go for the best, and I think I know why he was so shaken, so literally broken. I think he came to understand something he had not understood before, even with all of his knowledge of history; I think he came to understand, intimately, what the past was, and what it entailed.

6

"**A**ND THE BIBLE says this. . . . And the Bible says that. . . . And the Bible says this. . . . And when God says that, he *means* it!"

Moto said, "So what you're saying is that maybe you'll get to heaven with the right attitude."

"It's all right here." And Rank bipped his Bible with the back of his hand.

I looked down at Moto in his bunk and winked. Ford had his back to us, pretending sleep. I saw him flinch every time Rank interchanged the words "Bible" and "God." I don't think Ford could believe what had happened to him. His mother was born again during our junior year of high school, and after two years of prayer discussions and pamphlet giveaways and door-to-door "Are you saved?" drives he had hoped college would help him escape it all. But here was Rank, born again in half the time it took Ford's mom. She would call every Sunday night and talk to Ford for three or four minutes and then spend the next half hour on the phone with Rank. He was an in-house spy sanctioned by one of our own mothers. We had driven a thousand miles to find him.

Rank sat at his desk, Bible open, smiling that intensely broad smile peculiar to any ardent hobbyist who has suddenly been asked to share his vast untapped knowledge of his subject. He could have been a stamp collector or a World War I model-airplane enthusiast. What Rank wanted was another question, a little doubt to dispel. He was waiting patiently on us. Moto and I glared at each other and turned over. Rank closed his Bible and gushed

48

a sigh that whipped up all the sin in the room and left it hanging in the air atomized, bare dust motes, which nevertheless drifted down upon us during the long night. He opened his closet, put on his pj's, brushed his hair, and went to bed.

Moto and I finished out the evening with a Virginia conversation. He'd had his third note date in a month and was fast becoming, in his words, an expert on the American Breast. Virginia, who was a free spirit, a naturalist, a sharer, and a profound Darwinist, was nevertheless only these things from the belly button up. Ford had suggested that in their next encounter Moto might lose all remembrance of the existence of his hand, and where it would then fall he couldn't be held responsible for. Moto had forgotten to forget, or rather, hadn't the courage to forget. "She would start screaming and call the police, and there I'd be with my hand, forgotten, yes, but still attached to my wrist." So he had continued his breast dissertation and was, after all, highly contented with that, blessed, almost.

We lay and listened to Rank's prayers as he listened to something called "Gospel Images." He prayed for such a long time that I felt myself numbing into sleep, giving into it, when something pricked me, brought me back off the edge. I leaned out over the side of my bunk and looked down. Ford was there, standing over Rank, one arm pinning Rank's shoulder to the mattress. Ford whispered to him, a whisper like the hiss of boiling water spilled over flesh, whispering this, "Don't you pray for me, okay? You got that? I don't want you praying for me." I saw Rank nod, wide-eyed. "Okay?" Ford whispered. Rank nodded again. I rolled back over, as quietly as I could, and watched Ford walk back across the room and climb into his bunk. He lay on his back. And I lay on my back, and I suppose Rank was still on his back, and I don't think any of us rolled over for a long time.

*　　*　　*

I awoke the next morning remembering screaming and was awakened from my remembrance by screaming; there was screaming everywhere and so I screamed too. And amid this the writhing of bodies in the darkness, the clanging of bells, pounding feet, more screams and mangled curses, and then a pause, a quiet, and ants were singing, "Carry me down to the river, sweet Jesus, baby Jesus, throw me a lifeline when I'm there," and somebody yanked the cord out of Rank's earphones.

The pledges had finally struck, and we rang like a bell. Part of their requirement for initiation was a raid on the Fraternity House, wherein they'd do as much temporary damage to the house as possible and run like hell. If we caught just one of their number within the twenty-four hours following the raid, they all had to return to the house and clean up their mess and otherwise repent of their foul deed. If they escaped, and all they had to do to give us notice of a raid was ring the upstairs dinner bell, they could blaspheme for the rest of the semester. The whole spectacle was designed to build brotherhood.

I woke up when they rang the raid bell and remembered screams from the evening before, when our house cook, Jeanine, had found our stolen underwear in her walk-in freezer. They were, all one hundred and eighty-six pairs, frozen solid in a ten-gallon bucket of water. It was a solid block of underwear, and had been for some thirty-six days. Jeanine had taken the lid off expecting to find chicken parts. She had come into the dining room screaming, "Foul, foul, foul; get them foul things out of my kitchen." Wyeth took the job of thawing them out. Everyone but Wyeth had finally given in at one time or another, gone out and bought new underwear. He still had the one pair he was wearing when the others were stolen. It took him three hours to melt the block, and some ten minutes to sort his own out of the pile. He was very happy, and marched right down the hall to wash them.

And then I was awakened from my remembrance with more screams, the pledges escaping down the hall outside our door. I jumped down from my bunk then and landed squarely on top of Rank, who was crawling out of his bunk. I rode him as best I could till his legs gave out and we crumpled to the floor. I think Ford landed on Moto too. We all fell together in a great limb-entangling lump, knocking Rank's earphones off again, screaming and cursing, and when we all reached ground level and couldn't fall anymore, we were quiet and listened to gospel images. I still don't know who yanked the cord out of the stereo but I've got an idea.

I jumped up and turned on the light, and by that time the other three had a leg in their jeans and were hopping out the door after pledges. I grabbed a pair of shorts and the keys to the hearse. There must have been twenty guys in the hall trying to run and pull their pants on at the same time, leg out and elbows akimbo. We all jostled to the top of the steps at the same moment, and there stopped in mid-track. At the bottom of the staircase, in his fresh, clean pair of underwear and knocked coldly out, was Wyeth. He had gone after them, that hero, in his underwear, and the pledges, the scum, the bilge, had poured a gallon of maple syrup on the tile steps in their retreat. A couple of the guys tended to him and the rest of us ran on. The pledges had egged the foyer and shaving-creamed all the doorknobs, soaped the windows. We ran on outside, every loose gravel and blade of grass sticking to our pancake feet, and saw glimpses of skittering pledges round the corner of the house. After them. It seemed like the house was on fire. Every light was on and guys were piling out of every door and several of the windows. We beat it around the corner of the house, leading the charging horde, and almost ran over a Volkswagen bug. It was packed to the air vents with pledges. They screamed and pointed at us and the VW skidded, squalled, hunkered down and left, Ford sprawled spread-

51

eagle on its bulbous hood, face to face with pledges jammed against the windshield. That guy would tackle anything. Three minutes earlier he'd been asleep, and now here he was flinging himself onto the hood of a VW. How can you explain this? How can we expect anything? We ran after the VW for a few yards, and then turned and ran in the opposite direction for the hearse.

We caught them at the second stoplight. We were out of our minds with slapping ourselves on the back. We all jumped out and patted Ford on the shoulder and ringed the VW. Then the light turned, the bug sped away, and we were at a loss for words. We beat it back to the hearse and caught them again. The light changed as we were getting out and they sped away. This could go on all night. The pledges couldn't lose us; the hearse had too much speed. But we couldn't get at them. At every stoplight, eight of us would jump out and ring the VW and the pledges would scream and point at us behind locked doors and rolled-up windows till the light turned green and we had to run back to the hearse and give chase again. It was a nit contest, and we were winning. It was as exasperating as a toilet lid that won't stand up. It went on and on.

Moto said, "Is this all there is to life? Is this what the Big Bang leads to?"

But we figured they had to get gas, food, go to the bathroom at some time or another. So we followed.

There weren't many people on the road, the pledges had struck around two, but when we joined a third car at some intersection we noticed that the people thought it odd when eight guys in only jeans and shorts jumped out of a hearse and surrounded a VW, trying to open its doors, take off its tires, pick it up, et cetera, and then, as the light turned, give up all hope and race back to their black hearse. Some kind of roving mechanic's death squad. "We work on your car from our hearse as you drive to work. Night shifts only. Call us."

We chased them for over three and a half hours, through—and this is Moto's count—fifty-three stoplights, twenty-seven stop signs, one full-service gas station, one Burger Queen drive-thru, and one drive-in theater, where we watched part of *Mona Does* and the pledges tried to lose us by leaving during one of the best parts of Mona's doing. We drove by The Pancake & Egg Place, and although I didn't see the waitress, my whole body chilled at once with her memory.

It took the law to end it. At what must have been our fifty-fourth stoplight, the pledges took half a red light, and we would have taken a whole one in pursuit, followed suit; but a Lexington policeman trumped, slapped Jack perhaps, and pulled them over. That ended it. Any intervention by the Law in a raid automatically cancels any hope of its success. The pledges played by the rules, and, with their ticket in hand, followed us back to the Fraternity House.

They were a dismal, yet agitated, lot. They all had to go to the bathroom before clean-up began. Almost everyone in the house got up when we returned with our spoil. We slapped the pledges on the back, bemoaned a "good try," and handed them dishrags and mops. We clapped our hands and sang Fraternity songs while they cleaned. Wyeth had recovered and hopped among the pledges in his underwear, pointing out the error of their pledgely ways. By the time the pledges were through, every room in the house had been gone over, the tile floors mopped, waxed, and buffed, the carpet cleaned, and the fry grills and ovens in the kitchen scrubbed. All that was left was PT, physical training, about an hour of it, on the tile floor of the dining room, in their underwear. Ford was all too glad to lead the session. He started out with one-handed clapping push-ups, and three fat pledges knocked the wind out of themselves.

I couldn't watch. Memories of our own pledgeship the semester before came flooding back. So I volunteered to procure breakfast. It was a little something we did for the pledges after their workouts. I had been thinking of it all night. I gathered money to go to The Pancake & Egg Place for seventeen carry-out breakfasts. I jammed the dollar bills in my pocket (I'd showered and dressed while the pledges cleaned) and noticed myself scurrying toward the parking lot. And then I knew why. As I reached the door, Moto called after me, "Hart, I'll go with ya," and bounced after me.

And I don't know why it was, why I did it. I was tired and anxious and probably a little bit frustrated. Still, there wasn't any excuse for it. I turned around to Moto and said, "Why in the hell do you have to tag along behind me like some kind of damned kid?"

Moto stopped and looked down for a moment, then back up at me. He said, softly, "I don't," and turned away and walked away, back toward the dining room. I slammed the door behind me as I went out. There was no precedent for what I'd done, and Moto didn't deserve it. I was just anxious to go by myself. It was a rotten thing to do, the first truly mean thing I'd done to anybody outside of my family since I was a kid. I knew this and kept on walking.

And, of all things, she turned out to be there. I let the door close easily behind me and saw her out of the corner of my eye, and I immediately felt that what I'd done to Moto was all right. Her being there was worth, in some weird equation, what I'd done to him. The door closed behind me and I suddenly felt as if I were in over my head, and had been for too long. I had to do something to get out from under. I had to see it all the way through. It had been a long night; Ford had said what he'd said to Rank, and I'd said what I'd said to Moto, and it didn't seem, at the moment, that there was any going back. I slogged to the counter and sat down. It was still early, so there weren't too many people in the place. She moved along behind the stainless-steel counter toward me and I couldn't look up. I watched her white apron move toward me like the belly of a shark. I'd said that thing to Moto and I wanted to scream for it.

She said, "Do you want a menu?"

And I looked up and hiccuped out a "Yes, yes," and she kept moving along down the counter. Yes, I wanted a menu, I would have read Rank's *Concordance* straight through to stay the moment when I'd have to speak to her again.

She came gliding back and slid the menu to me, "There you go," and I nodded at her. The freckles were still there, lighter than I'd remembered, across the crest of her cheekbones and nose. Her eyes were some color I couldn't name but were definitely that color, some mixture of blue and green and gray, water at all seasons, that absorbed all the light in the room, and then sent it back out in shards whenever she glanced at something. Her hair, the color of a browned roll when you first open the oven door, was tied all in a bun except for two fine curls that fell down in front of her ears. She looked, I thought, as much as I could think, about twenty-seven or -eight. I looked for a ring but there wasn't any. The only jewelry she had on was a gold necklace with a pendant shaped in a musical note. It was a fine, thin, fragile note, that hung between the parted zipper of her smock against the pale V of flesh that was also, breathtakingly, mottled with the same faint freckles of her cheekbones. I could tell from twenty feet away that her breastbone was like a shell on the beach, like a skinny kid's in the summer; you could sound it with your knuckle and it would sing like a china plate. She was skinny all the way down to her hips, which flared just the slightest bit, and left her with, I imagined, what must have been a perfect pair of legs. And then there were black high-topped basketball shoes. They peeked out from underneath the hem of her bell-bottomed pant legs like twin Mercury outboards. I don't think I'd ever been more embarrassed. I felt like a kid watching a love scene on TV with my folks. I wanted to sink down between the cushions. I wanted to look for dimes and popcorn kernels. It was as if you'd put a pair of sneakers on Venus de Milo or the Statue of Liberty, or your mother. You just wanted to beat hell out of somebody for it.

She said, "Hi, what will you have?" and glanced at me and I thought, Well, this is it, I'm blinded, I'll never see again; somebody give me a stick.

"I need seventeen country breakfasts." And I pointed at the picture on the menu.

"What?"

"I need seventeen of these, to go." And she smiled. Okay, I thought, I'm willing to die now. And I smiled back, trying not to rip a corner of my mouth. "Really, I do; I need seventeen of them to go. Can you do that?"

"One guy walks in here and fills up the whole place. Yes, I can do it. It'll take awhile. You want something while you wait?"

"A Coke. I'll have a Coke."

"It's six-thirty in the morning."

"I've been up all night, I'll have a Coke." And she smiled at me again. I'd marry her and take my act on the road.

"Okay." And she kept on smiling and turned around and started the bacon. "You're one of those guys that showers in front of the whole campus, aren't you?" I stared blankly at her, then remembered I had my Fraternity jacket on. The ramifications of her statement almost brought tears to my eyes.

"You're a student?"

She turned around, still smiling. "Major of music. I walk past your house twice every morning. You guys harmonize pretty well for a bunch of naked guys."

I looked at her, my back arched, and said, "Music," and I coughed. "Music"—cough—"is my life." She stopped turning the bacon and laughed, held her palm to her

56

china breast and laughed out loud. I could have kissed myself for being so funny. She had the most perfect pair of lips I'd ever seen, stretched across square even teeth, that made my whole body lean forward. I put my elbows on the counter and almost toppled my Coke. She jumped forward to catch it, automatic waitress-reflex syndrome, but I beat her to it, widened my eyes, and it just made her laugh harder. She wiped her eyes and turned back around to the bacon and toaster. She got down seventeen Styrofoam trays and put the bacon and toast in them, and then started on the eggs. We hadn't said anything to each other in three or four minutes, and it was making me nervous again. I didn't want to flounder in the middle of it.

I grabbed the nearest piece of flotsam I had, said, "How do you work all night and go to school too?"

She looked at me and she wasn't smiling any longer. She paused. I was flailing at a board in the open sea, knocking it into splinters. And then she started to smile and drew it back and then offered it again, and before she could take it back I smiled at her, and then she let it come all the way. "It's not so bad. I work from twelve to seven, go back to the dorm and shower, go to my classes. I usually get through by twelve, and then I've got four or five hours to study before bed. It works out real well."

I said, "You're amazing." And then, "How long have you been doing that?"

"Since my first year—year and a half." And she grinned and turned back around. She was a sophomore. Probably nineteen or twenty. A year older than me, at least. She'd probably already noticed my two pimples; there was no getting around that, so I took my thumb and finger off them.

She cracked the eggs on the rim of the grill and had seventeen of them frying at once, and then another seventeen. She was remarkable. I closed the lids on the Styrofoam trays as she scooped the eggs into them. And then, as she was just turning over the last couple of eggs, one of them popped and she jerked her hand away and backed up, and before I could think I was around the end of the counter and by her side.

"You all right?"

And she looked up at me, startled that I was there. "Yes. It was just some grease on my finger." And she held it up, and there was a bright-red patch between two knuckles.

"That's gonna hurt," I said, and held my hands in front of me; for some reason they seemed totally useless appendages. "But I don't think you can do anything about it, really."

She said, "Yeah," and smiled, and scooped up the eggs, ladling them into the trays. I stacked them, and paid her, unwadding the bills from my pocket on the counter. She piled the trays in my arms like cordwood, till I was trays from waist to chin.

"Be careful," she said.

"Yeah." She held the café door open for me, and I wandered through it, brushing past her, wanting to trip.

And she stopped me with a hand on my shoulder. "Which car is yours?" And she kept on smiling, holding her bare arms in the cool March morning.

"That one, the hearse."

She looked at me, and looked at the ground, and looked back and said, "You come back."

"Sure," I said, and I started off for the hearse, my mind swimming, till I felt her breeze past me, to open the door.

7

W|E FOLLOW the creek till we reach the fence
line, tufts of dried grass hanging on barbed
wire, then wade through a shallow, wide place
in the stream, two inches of swift water over slate, and
crawl up the steep opposite bank, both of us on all fours.
There is a huge white sycamore at the crest of the creek
bank, alone among the black oaks and hickories. It hangs
out over the water. I look up into its branches, and look
at Zeke, and look up again. I am overwhelmed with the
possibilities of climbing this tree—shadow, dwelling,
flesh—and finally give in to the urge and leave the earth.
I grab hold of the lowest branch and pull myself up, and
then step up on another branch and swing over to another and pull myself up again. I am little of stature. I
have to climb. Christ might pass below at any moment.
And I wouldn't be able to see him for the press of my
own life. I rest for a while, a third of the way up the tree,
and look down at Zeke. He is looking up at me, his eyes
wide and ears cocked, amazed. I am a little flabbergasted
too; my head is light. I feel my toes bursting through the
ends of my sneakers and my pelvis shifting. I climb
higher, pushing through the leaves.

We are very late of the trees. It was just a season ago, a
leaf's fall from bough to ground. It's a safe place: You
don't have to glance over your shoulder, and very few
things on earth think of looking up. Someone might pull
that old joke on them, clip their nose. It's why we hide
the key over the door. Perhaps it is this remembrance of
our arboreal past that makes us climb trees when we're

59

kids, build tree houses. Perhaps it is why we are always trying to build taller, fly higher. A space station is only a higher, safer tree house. Pull up the rope, and even our own mothers can't get us.

I step up to another branch, and hug the trunk, inch around to a larger limb. Zeke is still below, far down below, waiting for me, gazing up. His neck must hurt. It was not so long ago that I'd be up here till he tired of the wait and wandered off after other prey. I look down again to see if there's any change in his temperament. He has lain down, his front paws *en croix*. I am in for a long wait. I break off a cluster of dried brown seed pods, hanging on doggedly from the fall before, and call it Arbor Day. I drop them through the branches at Zeke. One narrowly misses, but the second is on target and bounces off his shoulder. He jumps up and moves out into the sun, into safety.

I brachiate, higher and higher, and then suddenly almost lose my grasp, catch myself on a lower limb. My heart pounds and I hold on tightly for a moment. That old fear of falling. Our dreams remind us of it constantly. It might be our only inbred fear, falling; and maybe the darkness too, fear of that, our only true holdovers from a couple of million years back.

But it is not just these. It seems that everyone I know cringes when someone suggests cutting a tree down. Future first President or not, liar or honest kid, I'd still have busted him one for cutting that cherry tree down. A tree was planted at my birth, a pecan down in Fort Worth, that is still growing; my mother and father tend it. We fell for the Tree of Knowledge and were forced from Eden for the Tree of Life. It is our religious heritage, all dim memories of our lives eons ago. We were all Buddha under the bo tree; we were all Christ on the cross, the dogwood.

I look out, after climbing to the top, see the blue above the green, and the trees of the field clapping their hands.

I am, for a moment, omniscient, omnipotent. My fingers spread against the blue backdrop of the universe.

And then I notice a bird, a bird coast out of the sky and stall to a stillness on a branch across from me. He jerks his head around and the sun glances off his eye. He, sparrow, bird, is probably the principal living descendant of the dinosaurs. They roamed the earth, controlled it for over a hundred million years. We have roamed for perhaps five million and controlled only very lately.

Controlled, perhaps, not at all. I think about the life-born rock. I look beneath me and see that I am treed, forced into a hopeless situation. There is a theory: that we killed off the other protohumans. We were smarter, they scared us, and so, if we didn't club them, we didn't tell them that fire would hurt, either, and their species no longer exists. Australopithecines, Neanderthal, they didn't have a chance with us around. It's all coming back to us; it's all in the fossil record. And in our record too: Christ on the tree, the Holocaust, the nuclear weapon. And in my record too: what I said to Moto, among other things.

I pull my hand back down out of the sky, and look around me. The bird is gone, the visionary gleam is gone. And what of now, what now, if something were to run out of the woods, some protosapiens leftover, who had only half of my brain, but who could nevertheless swing a mean femur—what would I do? I would, I suspect, run, get my gun. It is, supposedly, what makes us unique, human: We anticipate our own deaths. It is not such a leap, anticipating this, knowing the rock and the bird, to anticipate the extinction of our species. It will one day be. The Negritos of the Philippines, the Andamanese, the Crow, the Blackfoot—tribes all over the planet buried and bury their dead in trees.

We have our limits. We can't live forever; we can't save a dying life no matter how much there is between us; we can't go faster than the speed of light; we can't make someone love us; and we can't change the past. And all these things are very trite, but they're relatively new to me, the silt of the last few years, a gradual acceptance, an evolution. I am different than I was before. We thought that if we learned how to climb a tree we could change the world; we thought it still when we climbed back down and sharpened a rock. Now we know better. Our only difference in being human is that we can ennoble our suffering. Sometimes I think it would be better just to suffer. I think I would rather howl at the moon.

But right here, now, I could look you right in the eye and smile. For God's sake, why? Why on earth? I look around me once more, and begin to climb down, a much slower process than climbing up. The twigs and leaves brush my arms and face as I drop, and I remember the beauty of the bird. My palms mold to the bark when I grasp and my arms flex as I swing. I hear Zeke moving about beneath me. Sap odor oozes through my nose. I swing onto the last branch and drop to the earth at Zeke's side, stand on my own two feet. He licks my hand. I look back up into the tree and suddenly couldn't care less. All of those things, the limits we have, are, after all, things we were born with; mean nothing in the moment that I breathe, reach down and scratch Zeke's skull. His itch overcomes all eternity. It is the very latest thing. I am, in my own way, the bird, a principal living descendant. I am suddenly brimming with responsibilities. We have our beauty too. Zeke and I, we set off up the hill at a jog. It's still early. There's still some work to be done. My father, when I was young and had been off climbing trees, would look down at me and say, "Son, where in the world have you been all this time!" And I would look up at him, agog, and smile. It's as early as it's ever going to be.

8

I WOKE UP in the middle of a street, in the middle of a night, car horns blowing and a crowd gathered around me. Ford was on one side of me and Moto on the other and we were being jostled forward by a huge shouting crowd, thousands around us, moving down the street and screaming, joined by hundreds more from side streets, dormitories, houses, restaurants and bars. It was as if at one moment the human species had finally decided enough was enough and was coming outside to do something about it. I expected to see water cannons and riot police at every turn.

A girl, with whiskers drawn under her nose and a pair of felt feline ears in her hair, stumbled past us and paused to scream, "Big Blue," and incidentally plumb Ford's throat in a spasm of pure human generosity.

"Ain't this great?" Ford yelled. "Bless her heart."

"She probably had a cold," Moto screamed back at him.

We moved along in the sea of humanity, drops of water that in the ocean searched for other drops. We passed by Kennedy's Bookstore and Holmes Hall, where a bunch of guys were hanging out of the windows on third floor rear. For a minute we stopped and looked up at them. We thought we might know them. But then the crowd pushed us along. We passed Blazer Hall, the Student Center, Memorial Coliseum, and finally arrived at the corner of Euclid and Woodland, where the whole campus had decided to converge at two in the morning. One guy jumped up on the roof of a car and Campus Security gingerly dragged him off. I could see their point, no use in being antagonistic about it, outnumbered three thousand to ten. There was a chant thronging through us. It picked up several houses, spun them, and set them back down perfectly on their foundations:

"We're Wildcats, we're Wildcats, and when we yell we yell like hell and this is what we yell: alabam, alabam, alabamdiego, San Diego, hocus-pocus, kiss my cocus, ra, ra, Wildcats."

We chanted it over and over. We thought it was an excellent chant. A couple of small, offshoot groups tried to get the school song going, or their sorority or fraternity chant, but they were quickly quashed and forced back into our chant. Every revolution turns eventually against revolutionaries.

The Wildcats had won. The University of Kentucky Wildcats Basketball team had won the NCAA championship. It was the best reason for a street party in a good while. Even though we realized we had little or nothing to do with the victory, we had roamed out into the night to celebrate it. Everyone was working through the crowd, congratulating one another, shaking hands, hugging. It was enough to make you think we actually liked each other. We had lost our inhibitions: bookworms danced under signal lights (primitive disco mirror balls), and homely people said, "Hi!?" and found that the word worked. Ford sang a country song. And I said, as the party was drifting off into subgroups—orgy gatherings, panty-raiders, car turner-overers, window breakers, test tomorrowers—I said, "Hey, you guys, I want you to meet somebody, meet Mary."

And they said, "Who?"

And I said, "Mary."

And they said, "Who?"

And I said, "Mary, this girl I've been seeing. I've told you about her."

And they said, "What?"

"Dammit, the girl at The Pancake & Egg. You remember. She found Moto's coat."

"What about her?"

"Well, I haven't actually gone out with her, but I've eaten there half a dozen times and talked to her."

"That's her job, she's a waitress," Ford said.

"Well, forget the whole idea," I said, disgusted.

Moto said, "Does an idea, a thought, have a chemical formula, a molecular makeup, that has to be broken down to be forgotten?"

"What?" I said.

"No, no," Ford waved, "let's go see her. That's where you've been going at midnight and six in the morning?"

"She works from twelve to seven, yeah. So what?"

"Nothing."

"Nothing at all about it," Moto followed.

"I still can't remember her," Ford said, "she must be something."

"You like a waitress?" Moto was just getting the idea.

"She's a student here, too," I said. "She's a music major. She plays the piano," I said, as we walked toward The Pancake & Egg.

"Why don't you want to take her out, though?" Ford asked.

"I want to," I said, "I just haven't asked her yet."

"We're not going to go through this again, are we," he went on.

"I just want you to meet her, damn it. I'll ask her out."

"Sure."

"She'll probably go out with you, Hart," Moto said.

"You guys just don't say nothing. We'll go in and have a Coke and come out. We'll just see her and I'll introduce you and you guys won't say anything."

"I'd rather go play some pinball," Ford said.

"You won't when you see her," I said, and we walked on silently. I realized I was taking an awful chance. I'd really lost all my inhibitions. Moto, of late, had been attracting girls at a precipitous rate, but they all had the same perplexed expression that he carried most of the time. That really wasn't what I was worried about. It was the thought that Mary might think I really cared, that since my folks weren't here I was introducing her to some odd set of surrogate parents, Ford and Moto. I mean she might think that I thought she was mine to show off already. Maybe I wanted her to think that.

We walked into the café, and were struck by the brightness of the place out of the night, and she was standing there behind the counter, and Ford and Moto both turned and looked at me, and—and I came out of the memory, woke fully, and was staring up at the ceiling, holding on to both edges of my mattress. I was sweating a little. I think I came out of the memory because I didn't want to remember.

It was now late in the morning, it was April, and we had our first date this afternoon. I'd asked her that night of the street party, after Moto and Ford had gone on. I'd gone out of the café with them and then come back in later, and she was clearly startled to see me again so soon. I went right up to the counter, still squinting and blinking from the glare of the lights and the stainless steel and said, with my palm standing on its edge on the counter, said, "Hi, look, this Saturday I'm going down to my grandfather's farm, and I'd like to take you to see it if you'd want to. I mean if you're free and can, want to." And I looked at her.

She said, "I'm free."

Just like that. "I'm free."

And she went on, "Can we go in the afternoon? I've got to work that morning, but I'm off Sunday morning, and it won't hurt if we get back late."

I didn't say a word, just nodded; just like Moto, I thought. I nodded and smiled and we set a time and I backed up all the way out of the café, and stumbled all the way back to the Fraternity House. The Wildcats had won the NCAA that night. It was nothing compared to what I'd just accomplished.

I'd seen her some before that night, since that first

morning when I'd bought the seventeen breakfasts. In fact, I went back to the café two days later, got up with Rank for his first class, and beat it across campus at six-thirty. I had a waffle and some orange juice, which she made a face at—how could I, she asked, stand the sweet syrup and sour juice together; didn't it twork my jaw?

And I had said, "Why do you wear high-toppers?"

And she had crossed her feet, one over the other, and said, "Why do you drive a hearse?"

"Cheap transportation," I said.

"Lousy ankles," she said.

"I'm sorry."

"No, they've always been that way. Born with 'em."

"What kind of music do you major in?"

"Where'd that come from?"

"It's just a question."

"I play the piano. Result of these ankles. Couldn't run around much when I was little."

"You don't like playing the piano? Your mother forced you to play the piano."

"What? I love the piano. You probably don't like it. Anybody who'd eat waffles with orange juice couldn't like the piano."

"I don't know anything about it."

"You should learn. I gotta go." And she was gone to another table. Her hair was still up in a bun and she wore the same brown-and-orange pant uniform. I ate my waffle slowly, watching her serve and talk and smile at the customers. They were older men mostly, guys who worked in the tobacco warehouses around campus and came in for coffee and a roll before work. I was the only person under thirty in the place, besides her. I finished at exactly seven, and wouldn't you know it, just as she was putting on a jacket and punching out. Another waitress took my money. Mary was at the cash register too, telling the new girl where she was with her orders. I waited till they were through to drag my change off the counter and button my jacket. She looked at me and said, "Can you speak? It tworked your jaw, didn't it, and now you can't talk. Your tongue's in knots."

I said, "How's your finger?"

It made her pause. She looked down, and held her finger up and looked at it like, well, it's true, I do have a hurt finger. "It's okay, I think. Still hurts to play, though. You drive your hearse over here?"

"No."

"Are you walking back to your fraternity house?"

"Yeah."

"Mind if I tag along? It's still a little dark out."

"No. Sure," I said.

"I'll be glad when the time switches back over."

"Yeah. Me too," and while I opened the door for her I praised Daylight Savings Time as a God, which wouldn't begin for another couple weeks, and which would make it even darker at seven. I'd never really consciously thought about it before, but she was shorter than me. By just about an inch or so. And she walked just like any normal-ankled person. We walked, and while she talked I bathed in the wonder of our walking together. She was from Colorado, had six brothers and sisters, all older, and hated The Pancake & Egg. It seemed an incredulous statement at the time, considering how much I'd grown to like the place. She worked there because she needed the money, she only had a partial scholarship, and because all the walking kept her ankles in shape. I'd never seen her on campus before because none of our classes were even remotely close to each other. Her dad and mom were sixty-one and fifty-eight, respectively, and still lived in Boulder, where he taught at the university and she ran a ski shop.

"I'm a major disappointment, although they hate to admit it. I couldn't ski for Mom, with my ankles, and I decided not to go to Dad's school. He's taught sociology there for twenty-six years." She must know all about sex

68

roles, I thought. I told her about Texas and Grandpa and his farm and Moto and Ford, and walked a hundred yards past the Fraternity House before she stopped me. I said, "Oh. Yeah. Bye."

"Bye."

And it was all I could do to get myself to turn around. As I walked back toward the house I ran through the seven or eight hundred things I should have told her about and in what tone of voice I should have told it to her in, and when I got up to the room and had stood in the middle of it for five minutes with my hands shoved in my pockets, I realized that I was already totally exhausted and the rest of the day was shot. I undressed and got back in bed.

A few days later, after I'd run around town in the hearse like some kind of inspired Liberace, I met her again. At seven in the morning I pulled my box, a purchase that had required three days of searching, out of the bottom of my closet and went out front of the Fraternity House to the hearse and crawled in through the back door, the casket door. I lifted the lid on the box and took out the miniature plastic baby grand piano and snapped the legs in. Then I played a few notes of "Chopsticks." There had been a "Learn the Piano by Numbers" booklet in the box, and I had spent half of the night before in the back of the hearse learning the tune. I used the "one-finger" approach, as opposed to the more difficult "two hands, four-finger" method. I didn't have that much time. I picked up the piano, and the little piano stool, and backed out of the hearse. The car was nose-in to the sidewalk, so I just set the piano and its little plastic stool on the hood, leaned on the fender facing in the exact opposite direction she'd be coming from, and waited. It couldn't be too long. I'd show her what I'd learned. I thought that this was probably the cutest thing anybody could ever do. I folded my arms.

There were a few people out, but not many, so when

they passed I just looked the other way. If I was lucky, no one I knew would come along. The Fraternity House didn't usually wake up till about seven-thirty. She would be along a good ten minutes before then. I waited and I waited.

Seven twenty-five. Seven-thirty. Seven thirty-five. Where was she? Damn, it pissed me off. And as I shifted my feet I heard a *pink-pink* and turned around, expecting to have to chew some clod out for fooling with my piano. But it was her. *Pink-pink,* she went again, striking the plastic ivory. She was looking at the keys with an intensity that I hadn't counted on. She tapped out a few more notes with her index finger, then put her pocketbook on the hood of the hearse so she could get both hands on the thing. She didn't say anything or even look at me. I'd paid twelve bucks for the goddamned thing. She hit a few more keys, using the two-hand, ten-finger method, and all of the sudden it wasn't *pink-punk-pink* anymore; it was some kind of classical thing, Bach or Beethoven or something like that, your real complicated-looking-on-a-page stuff. I looked down, amazed. She finished and looked up at me and smiled. I said, "Can you play 'The Sting,' from that movie with Robert Redford?"

"That's 'The Entertainer,' by Scott Joplin. Yeah." And she put her fingers on the keys, softly, the way you might touch a pot to see if it's hot, moving in slow and then finding the pot is cool and your heart beating again. She played it fine, all the trills and brittle parts the same, just made up of *pinks* and *punks* and *ponks.* Then she quit and picked up her purse and said, "Can I borrow this?"

I said, "Yeah, sure," and then she picked it up and walked off without even a thanks.

A few feet away she turned and, while backing up, said, "I'll bring it back to you. Promise."

"Okay." I was still leaning against the fender. I'd had no idea it would work that well. It was the best twelve-dollar investment I'd ever made. I watched her walk off

70

in her brown-and-orange uniform, and then I skipped back down the sidewalk and into the house.

This was all the week or two before the NCAA street party. We had stepped into the café that night, Moto and Ford and I, and she was there behind the counter, like a waterfall. Everything was sparkling—the toaster, the counter, the salt-and-pepper shakers. She was, from the first, a little nervous. She mouthed a "hi," instead of saying it, and took to wiping the counter. I ushered Moto and Ford into a booth. We sat for a while and finally she came over.

"Hi," I said.

"Hi."

"Mary, this is Moto." And I threw my thumb toward him. "And this is Ford."

"Hi. I've heard a lot about you guys." And then she jerked out her pad. Moto and Ford couldn't have possibly gotten a word in. "What would you like?" What was wrong with her? She wasn't supposed to be nervous with new people, she was a waitress. I'd never seen her nervous before. She stared intently down at her pad, pen ready. I noticed she had one foot on top of the other.

"Cokes," I said, "just three Cokes."

She wrote it down, said, "Got it," and turned and left.

"Hey," I yelled after her. I was nervous now. "What's wrong?"

She turned around and she was mad when she said it, or mad and hurt. "Nothing." Like I'd kidded her for crying at a movie or something.

We drank our Cokes, and she stopped by once to ask us why we were out so late, and we told her, and she said, "Oh," and went on. I paid for the Cokes and she smiled at Moto and Ford and said, "It was nice meeting you," and turned, as quickly as she had before, to the counter. It was terrible. Whatever was going on was terrible. My throat was all dammed up.

71

We walked out of the café and started back toward the Fraternity House.

"She's real pretty, Hart," Moto said.

I didn't even want to nod. I don't know why I wanted them to meet her. I was just so damned proud of her. Not just because I knew her and she had smiled at me. I was proud of the whole world just for her.

Moto had caught my mood pretty quick. He said that one thing and then kept quiet. Ford, I guess, was still thinking about the girl with the Wildcat ears. He was hopping around, jamming his hands in his pockets and dragging them back out, whistling.

"Pretty," he said, "but a little flighty. What's her major?"

"Piano," I said. I wanted to punch him for the mood he was in.

"Piano? What can you do with that when you graduate? And where'd she get them clodhoppers? I thought I'd bust a gut."

Moto still didn't say anything. I didn't want to say anything, but Ford was looking at me as we walked. "She wants to play and compose. She's good," I said. I didn't know if she was really any good or not. I just said it. It didn't matter. I didn't say anything about her ankles.

We walked on a bit further, and Ford was starting to calm down a bit, had jammed his fists into his jeans pockets and left them there, when he sighed and said something all of us had said before in passing; it was a joke. He said, "Well, I'd fuck her."

It just sort of washed me away, what he said. I turned while we walked, grabbed the front of his jacket with both hands, and gave him a good running shove. He still had his hands in his pockets or he might have caught himself. As it was, he stumbled and fell backward over a low bush and hit the ground with a thud. As soon as he got his hands out of his pockets he was up and back over the bush.

72

"What the hell was that for?" He was surprised and a
little scared, I think. I was just standing there, panting,
my arms at my sides. It seemed like I was just empty. I
turned and put my hands in my jacket and walked the
other way.

"What the fuck's wrong with you?" Ford yelled.

I heard Moto tell him to leave me alone. I don't know.
I didn't look back. I broke out in a trot and ended up
running all the way back to Mary at the café. I can remember the wind in my eyes. I went back to the café and
walked in, blinded, to the counter and asked her, and she
said, "I'm free." I'm free. She told me later on that she'd
been so nervous when Ford and Moto came in with me.
"I was so nervous," she said. She'd known, she said, how
much I cared about them, and how much they meant to
me, and how at the time she'd been so jealous of them,
and wanted, at the same time, for them to like her. Well.
It was a stupid thing I'd done, shoving Ford. Not only for
the fact that he could have killed me with one arm if he'd
wanted to. I apologized a couple of days later, and he
looked at me and nodded, shrugged his shoulders.
Christ.

It was Saturday, and I'd slept late, and I only had about
two hours to get ready, wash the hearse, and pick Mary
up. I'd called Grandpa and told him we'd be down
around three or four. I thought he'd kid me about her,
but he sounded pleased and said, "Come on."

I jumped out of bed, dressed, washed the hearse inside
and out, showered, dressed again, and had an hour and
fifteen minutes to wait. I sat on my bed. I looked at the
clock. I went downstairs and fixed myself a bowl of cereal
and read the paper. Only fifty minutes left to wait. I figured it would take me five minutes to walk outside, get in
the hearse, and drive to the Tower, the new skyscraper
dorm. Mary was on the fifteenth floor. It'd take a couple
of minutes to ride the elevator up to her room. All this

figuring took one minute, so I only had forty-nine minutes left to go. I could feel myself sweating all over my clothes. But the time finally passed. I watched TV for a while, went upstairs and combed my hair again.

Moto said, "Big-Date Kid."

Rank asked if I wanted to borrow his brush.

Lord, I thought, I'll never do this again as long as I live.

It was the fastest elevator I'd ever been on in my life. I thought I'd have a good couple of minutes to calm down as I went up, but the elevator had me at the fifteenth floor in about eleven seconds. The doors sucked back and I stepped out; the doors slammed shut and the elevator went back down. I had been spit out like a seed. I wandered the hallway, a scrap of paper in my hand with Mary's room number on it, though I knew it by heart. Number 1528. There it was, staring right back at me. She had a little chalkboard on her door for messages when she was out. The chalkboard was orange and in the shape of a cat's head. You were supposed to write in the cat's wide white Cheshire smile. I thought about leaving a message and leaving. But I stood at the door and knocked, and the door was opened unto me.

And what I saw I did not expect. The only time I'd ever seen Mary was at The Pancake & Egg Place, or on the way from there. I expected to see her in her brown-and-orange uniform, with her hair in a bun. I was looking at another person. This girl had shoulder-length auburn hair, full of body and brushed back over one ear. There were tiny diamond studs in her lobes. She had on a plain tan cotton jacket, but her blouse was some kind of a mixture of cotton and silk, high-collared with lots of pleats, the kind girls usually wear a little black ribbon with. But Mary didn't have the ribbon. The blouse was left open at the neck, and open for another button below that. She was an oasis. I was poured out like water. She had on a pair of faded jeans that fit tightly at the ankle,

74

and a pair of sparkling white high-topped sneakers. She had dressed up for me.

"Ready?" I said, backing out into the hall.

"Ready," she said, and closed the door behind her.

I am at a loss. I remember dropping out of the sky as I had risen. And I must have walked to the hearse and driven it to Grandpa's. That would have taken a good hour. But all I really remember as we moved is the blur of the world that was not her face. No, I remember more. I remember thinking that somehow she was uncomfortable with the way the world was fixed. In the hearse she rolled down windows, shoved aside curtains, and the wind billowed in on us and our conversation. Every once in a while she would have to push her hair back around behind her ear. She couldn't seem to sit still, or just sit and look forward. She brought one ankle up underneath her and put her back to the door and looked at me. On the Bluegrass Parkway, we saw a hitchhiker up ahead, and watched him jerk his thumb behind his back when we approached. He didn't want a ride from a hearse. It made her laugh. She laughed and laughed, and every once in a while after that I would look over and she would still be smiling.

The blur of the world that was not her face. I have caught a leaf, a feather, and a snowflake as they fell out of the sky. It was all like this somehow, being with her, the moment you realize it might fall into your hand, and then the beauty of it resting there in your palm afterward. Such a feeling of being given something. Without asking for it or even knowing it was ever there, existed at all.

Grandpa was out in the side yard when we pulled up. He, too, was not the person I knew. Clean-shaven, in a white shirt and an old pair of gray slacks; he smoothed his hair back when we got out. He was on Mary's side of the car, so I rushed around to stand by her. I couldn't understand why she wasn't as shocked as I was. I looked

75

at him with a skeptic's eye and he just refused to acknowledge my stare.

I said, "Grandpa, this is Mary," and, "Mary, this is my
grandfather, Gude Scatter."

She held out her hand and said, "Why, hello, Gude,"
and shook his hand and turned him toward the house all
at the same time. He was just another old guy in for a
coffee. It was as if she were his age, with all its rights.
She'd called him Gude.

We went in the house, after she met Zeke and shook
his paw too, and sat at the linoleum table. Grandpa sat
across from Mary and me.

He said, "How are you, son?" and lifted his hand toward my dazed skull.

I shied, but all he did was stroke my cheek and draw
his hand back. What was going on here? He and Mary
did most of the talking, about the difference between
Colorado and Kentucky mountains, the kinds of soil and
trees; how the weather was back in Colorado now; what
her dad did; what she did; what she wanted to do. They
were completely infatuated with one another. I was completely nervous. I was proud and jealous all at the same
time. Grandpa made some tea and we all moved out to
the front porch. I sat on the swing at one end, and Mary
and Grandpa sat in rockers at the other. I could barely
hear their conversation, much less enter it. What could
they talk about? He was an old man and she was a pianist.
I turned to watching the wind blow through the trees.
They talked and they talked. After an hour or so I figured he knew more about her than I did. But for some
reason, out on the porch, my nervousness went away, and
I felt very safe. I swung on the swing and watched the
trees.

Finally, I felt a lull in their talking, and felt Grandpa
rising out of his rocker with a little roar. He moved to the
front door, stopped, looked around, and said, holding his
chest, "Why, it's so crowded out here, you couldn't cuss a

cat for getting hair in your mouth." Patted his chest and went inside. Lord.

I looked at Mary and smiled. I went across the porch, totally confident, and held out my hand. She took it and I pulled her out of the rocker, holding on to her as long as possible before letting go.

"C'mon," I said. It was beginning to get dark. We stepped off the porch and I guided her in the direction of the pond, had put my hand on the small of her back to squeeze between two trees, when Grandpa stepped out on the front porch again and called after us.

"Do you like pork chops, Mary, honey?"

And she said, "Yes, but you don't have to cook for . . ."

I poked her in the ribs. "Yes, I like them."

"Okay," he said, "y'all come back in a little while then."

I nodded at him and pushed her on.

"Be careful," he yelled after us.

Mary smiled, just barely raised the corners of her lips. "He likes to cook," I said. "If he didn't cook for me and Moto and Ford every once in a while, he'd just eat break-fast three times a day."

We walked out of the yard and across a small field to the pond behind the house. It was full, brimming with spring, and a good trickle ran over the spillway. We walked around it, looking in the water, chasing a V-shaped school of mallard chicks around and around, chunking rocks at turtle heads. Zeke found us, that male-factor, and ran around and between us, flogging us with his long tail, and then kept shoving his snout at Mary's crotch. She was so embarrassed she sat down on the grassy bank of the dam. I sat by her, and patted Zeke, and so did she, and then I let him gnaw on the toe of my sneaker. And we were quiet. We watched the night fold over the pond, and the ducks wobble out of the water on the far side to roost among the rushes. I threw a rock out into the middle of the water and we watched the ripples it made, all the way into the bank where they became tidal waves to an ant. And we watched the water calm, as if nothing had ever been. We chewed on blades of grass and just watched.

She said, "I like him. He's cute. I think you look like him. You know what you'll look like when you're old."

I wanted to hug her. I had always thought we looked alike, me and that old man, but no one else had ever seen it, said it.

"I think he is the best person I have ever known," I whispered. It was dark and the baby ducks were huddled around the mallard trying to sleep.

"He talked to me about his wife." And she was whispering too.

"She died almost thirty years ago. I never met her." And this was about all I knew of her from my grandfather. My mom had told me the little I knew.

"He told me about how she loved music. How she would move through the house humming or singing. He said he would come in at any time during the day and hear her, somewhere in the house all alone, humming and singing to herself. He would wander from room to room looking for her as quietly as he could, stopping and listening, and then going on till he found her, at whatever she was doing. And how she would always stop when he came in the room, when she noticed he was there. Sometimes, he said, he would stand outside the door and listen, looking down at his boots."

I looked at her.

She said, "Can you imagine?"

I think my eyes must have been all mussed up because she said, whispered, "Aw, Hart," and put her hand on my arm.

"I'm sorry," she said.

"No," I whispered. I was so sad I almost couldn't bear it. I just kept thinking and thinking about it and at the same time I had this picture of him in my head frying an egg for himself. Jesus, I was a sentimental jerk.

78

I got a little better and said, "No," again, and then went on. "He was in World War I. He was a regular goddamned foot soldier in the trenches. I mean, he used to stand in them trenches and look out over the dirt at the enemy and every once in a while shoot at them with his gun. A gun. Can you imagine," I said. "On the first day of the last spring of the war, when it was all starting to end, he was still in a trench, looking out over the dirt. And out of nowhere somebody shot him. Shot him in the back, in the shoulder, and he spun around with the force of the bullet and pulled his trigger and knocked a vertebra out of the back of a German's throat who was standing up on the bank of the trench. He says it was all reflex. Didn't hardly know what he had done. He picked up the German's helmet as a souvenir before they buried the guy. He's still got it. Carried it home across the Atlantic in his duffel bag. He still has a little mark on his shoulder too. Whenever it's in the news he'll tell me how much he hates wars, and how he'd sit in the middle of a field with a sandwich—let them take all the rest, if they just won't have the war."

We got up and walked down toward the barn. I led the way because it was dark, led the way holding her hand for a hundred yards before I realized what I was doing. God, I had a lot of gall. And then I remembered she hadn't taken it away. I couldn't, at that moment, have counted my own fingers and toes. I opened the gate that led into the barnyard and led her through.

"I'll close it," she whispered.

"No," I said, "a good cowboy always closes a gate he opens."

It was getting a little cold out, and I felt her warm breath on my cheek as I reached past her to latch the hasp. It sent a shudder through me that the earth must have felt. I let go of her hand and skipped up the little hill toward the barn. It was cold and clear out, black, black, black, but for the nail holes in the sky.

"Hart?" she said.

"C'mon."

She caught up to me. The porch light on the house twinkled off the diamond in her ear. I led her through the small door next to the big sliding one, and we entered into the warmth and secrecy of an animal's burrow. I expected to run up against some old fur, or a rabbit's bones at each step. I started to climb up the ladder, when she caught me by the belt loop on the back of my pants and pulled me back down.

"Are you going to show me the new hay?" I could feel her smile. And I think I would have kissed her then if I could have seen her.

"No," I whispered, "just follow me up the ladder." One of the horses snorted at us then, banged against the side of its stall, and it made her reach out and touch my jacket. "Okay," I said, "you go first then. Be careful." I guided her to the ladder and up she went. I followed her up and took her hand again, and felt my way to the loft door. It was blacker up there than when you first turn out the lights. I bumped into an old barrel and a bale of hay, but we finally made our way, and I swung out the old door to the view of the dark farm. I sat down against one side of the opening, with one leg dangling out into the barnyard, and she sat against the other. I pointed out the dim outline of the hills, where the stars stopped, and the faint dawnlike glow of Decatur in the distance. The little porch light shone against the underside of the branches of the trees in the front yard, and we watched the empty swings and rockers sway in the wind. The lights in the kitchen were on, and Grandpa moved slowly back and forth past the windows. A car passed, slow and rumbling, down along the road. We watched it for the mile of its tortuous passing.

"It's wonderful here," she said softly. "It's just wonderful."

Her hair had fallen in front of her ear on that one side, and so I reached over and pushed it gently back behind.

And then she said it again, "Aw, Hart," like she was giving up. And I looked at her whole face, glancing down at her lips and chin, till I finally had to look away. And then I felt her moving, and I turned back to her, and I sat there with my head against the wood of the door and waited for her, as she leaned across the infinite space of eighteen inches, to kiss me. And she did that, and drifted slowly back to her doorpost and rested there, looked out again at the dark farm. And so I leaned over then, leaning over to pick up a leaf in a windstorm, leaned forward to her across that piece of night.

9

O N THE WAY back to the tractor a rabbit bursts out of the high fescue in front of us and we are all three thrust immediately into the thick of life, the food chain. "Take, eat; this is my body," the rabbit says. Zeke nearly quarters himself trying to get started after that rabbit. He is on the trail before the tall hay can sway back over the rabbit's wake. It was a low blur of brown and pure white and then a blotch of black and then a calm screen of hay before me. I say, "Hey!" and take off, following the aerial of Zeke's waving tail. "Hey!" I say again, and leap after them, or rather, after Zeke, who's after the rabbit, who's after who knows what, his own life. I jump through the high hay, spreading it with my arms as I run, yelling. We run over one hill and down into another hay field and under a fence into a thicket of bois d'arc. Zeke ousts the rabbit from there and we are off again. I am breathless. It is their job to run, not mine.

We run over the curves of the earth, a man chasing a dog chasing a rabbit.

What if, at this moment, the earth's magnetic field flips, as it does every half a million years or so, and south becomes north? Would we, all three, pause, and then turn in the other direction, rabbit chasing dog chasing man? It has been seven hundred thousand years since the last flip. We are overdue. Suddenly, I stop. Zeke has stopped. Lord, this is it. Run for your life. Where is my burrow? We've been talking with our mouths full of rabbit for seven hundred thousand years. I feel like a blade of grass, or a dog bone. Zeke stops, and I stop, and then he does a series of long high smooth leaps, grand jetés, followed by a couple of *changement* moves, jumping straight up and turning 360 degrees on the way down, all the while looking for the rabbit. He's lost him. He looks some more, but his tail is down now, so I have to look for the furrow in the grass to track him. I finally find him sniffing around a pile of rocks and say, "Give it up." He looks up at me and wipes the saliva off the rim of his mouth with his tongue. "Fair and square," I say. His tongue hangs out like an empty palm. "C'mon, I'll feed you." And we start again for the tractor we left with the cows. We have been gone so long, they've probably talked it into coming over to their side. It's already been eating grass since the day it was born.

But it is still there, docile in the field. The cattle graze about it, whispering. I move through them and they yank their heads up and out, playing dumb. Zeke and I climb aboard and rumble out of the herd. It is now long past noon and we are thoughtless but for sustenance. We hurry through the gates and bounce over ruts down into the barnyard and under the tractor port. It seems ages since we were here this morning. I let Asia out of her stall into the barnyard to get some exercise while Zeke and I go up to the house for lunch. Zeke's tongue is still watering the earth. He looks up at me as we walk. I look back at him. What do we care? Let us eat and drink; for to-morrow we shall die.

I stop off at the chicken coop, grab a little fat of the land, and cradle the three eggs in my shirt front. Zeke moves up behind me as I back out of the coop and I fall backward over him. Save two eggs with my two hands and the third—I watch it in slow motion—rises but peaks soon and fails to bounce. So much wasted chicken effort. I scratch my head. I will never be President that way, I think.

Zeke licks up what he can and I carry the other two eggs into the house. Zeke wants to come in too, but I don't let him. Instead I pick up his huge plastic bowl and fill it with dog food and set it in front of his drooping face. "You're a dog," I say, somewhat guiltily, "act your part." He looks at me as if I'm asking the lion to eat straw. I fill up his water bowl and go back in the house without looking at him again. I think the big brown eyes of a bird dog have evolved concurrently with the human conscience.

I step into the house, let the door close softly behind me, and stop to listen for the woman I never met. I listen for the music of my grandmother in this old house. I wander from room to room, up the stairs and through the two big bedrooms there. I open every closet door and poke my head up into the attic. And although the pipes shudder and the stairs creak and I can hear the wind fizzing through the house, I hear no humming. No one sings, no matter how hard I gaze at my boots. Maybe she has always known I was there. I am not nearly subtle enough. The noise of my hope deafens the place.

I clop back downstairs to the kitchen, turn off the light I left on this morning. It is less than a rock tossed in the pond. The eggs are balanced on the counter, and the frying pan from this morning is still on the stove, so I see that I am determined to have an egg sandwich. And as I run water over the skillet and begin to wipe it dry, I hear a voice. It comes out of the radio, only a couple of words I can't quite make out, and then it's quiet again. The voice broke out into the room as if someone had just spit out a gag and screamed. It came from the radio that was on, but the volume was all the way down. It was, I realize, someone on a CB in a car passing on the road. There are voices everywhere waiting for their chance. I think about flipping the tuner for my grandmother's humming.

I had no right. I had no right to feel sorry for my grandfather there on the bank of the pond with Mary. He was a strong, happy man who'd chosen his life after my grandmother died. He was, I think, always tuned in. That night, after he fed us, I drove us home. Mary said, her head on my shoulder and her feet up against the windshield, "Maybe we could watch out for each other. Maybe we could, you know, keep an eye out."

I turn my eggs over, break the yolks. We are what we eat; so I eat my heart out. No one need send an eagle to pluck my organs daily. Everything I've ever done was self-inflicted. I'm an auto-cannibal. Somebody give me a napkin, I keep missing my mouth.

I drove back to the Fraternity House that night, after rising to the fifteenth floor with Mary, and falling down, and Ford was still up. He was studying at his desk, the lamp a circle of light on his book and hands.

"How'd it go?" he said.

"It went well, my friend. She kissed me."

"Really? Gosh, that's great, Hart." And he turned out his light and we went to bed. Before I slept I looked over at him, lying on his back. I remember now, not the darkness of that night, but of the other, when he had risen to whisper to Rank. I remember that distinctly. I remember the long intervals of darkness between headlights running our windows around the upper walls of the room. And when they would come, the rushing panes of light, I would look over and see Ford still lying on his back.

We are all born lovers; our only problem is remaining that way in the face of so many obstacles. I fix my sandwich and get myself a big glass of water, sit down to my long overdue lunch.

It is so quiet here. Where is the humming?

I don't know if it will help. I have eaten the air, promise-crammed. I don't think I need it now. I did eat. But if you want to, you can say a prayer for me.

10

I T LOOKED to me like somebody snorted a bottle of ink and then sneezed. It was that random. But then I could see a measure in the madness, something linear and sometimes repetitive. Still it seemed hieroglyphic, unbreakable code, print to the blind. I had to hear it to understand. I didn't believe a note of it. I handed the sheet music back to her and told her I didn't speak much music, much less read it. I was strictly a silent partner.

We walked, hand in hand, Mary and I, along a carpeted hallway, stopping at each cell and peering in through the small, thick pane of glass. It was a busy night. Almost all of the padded rooms had someone in them. There must have been a full moon or something, maybe Lyra bright overhead. Mary finally found a vacant room and we ventured in of our own free will. There was carpet on the floor here too, and the walls were padded in the same brown burlap fabric as the other rooms we'd passed. It became very quiet when the door closed on the hall. Mary sat me down on the one chair in the room, put her purse in my lap, kissed me on the nose. I sort of felt like a puppy. Then she spread her music out on the piano, and sat down. It was this great big three-legged black piano, a grand, that took up the whole room. I was squeezed in a corner, my legs under my chair, clutching Mary's purse. How did they get it through the door? They must have built it there. The chair I sat in was a complete afterthought. They hadn't planned on anybody, in these padded-for-quiet practice rooms, actually wanting to listen.

The music was something she'd written for a class. Before she started she took a breath and reached up with both hands and pushed her hair behind her head, held it up there for a moment and then let it all fall back. I'd never seen anyone so serious with a moment. Her lips were parted, breathing and trembling; she slid her palms along the top of her thighs, drying the sweat. Okay. She left one hand on her thigh, arched her back slowly and just a bit, and placed the fingertips of the other hand on the keyboard. But only one finger moved, sharply and stiff, and this is how the music began.

Hers was the only sound in the world.

A single note, like a drop of water on the bottom of a pot in the middle of the night, poignant, metallic; and the only thing left for your life is the length of the moment before the next drop. Her fingers were all slightly above the keys now, spread and quivering, and then, like a bird jerking his head around, she hit the note again, and again there was the space of night where you're waiting, and then she did it again, and then again, and finally she raised her other hand from her thigh and placed it above the keys too, and you knew immediately that it might never stop raining, that you should have fixed the roof long ago, and that there's not enough pots and pans and buckets in the world to catch it all now, so you might as well lie there and let it come. And it came. She let her fingers fall to the keys. Please. And it rolled off the roof amid the drops in the pots and plopped in a pool outside the window. It rippled and lifted a leaf and carried it off like a fallen hero, shoulder-high, through bowing blades of grass. And it rained harder. Please. The water rose, crept in over the sill, and soon the bed and the rest of the furniture were floating, bumping around the four walls. A trout jumped across me, a tiny rainbow. I pulled my sheets up under my chin. I looked out the window and understood that the whole house bumped around the four walls of the world, that we were all being carried away. Her hands moved from one end of the keyboard to the other, sounding thunder and pitch and flashes of lightning, thrashing, and then, at its worst, when all the oxygen had been used up from the last air bubble trapped high in the corner of the room, and you begin to sink, amazed, she stopped. Limbo. Sustained. Living on your last gulp. Quiet. And out of nowhere, waking up from a dream, the single note again, just the one hand quivering above the keys. And then once more, to let you remember. It was like this.

And she sat there for a moment, sweat on the bridge of her nose and upper lip, running her palms along her thighs. She turned to me.

"I don't think I'm going to play it again. I was going to play it twice for practice, but I don't think I'm going to play it again tonight."

I was sitting in the chair, both of my legs tucked up under me, her purse in my lap. I got up and sat next to her on the bench and gave her a hug. She was still trembling, somehow very weak, even though every muscle in her body was taut.

"You sure hug a lot," she said.

"I'm sorry." And I leaned back a little.

Then she shook her head, and said, "No." I'd sat down straddling the piano bench, and as she said, "No," she got up and straddled it too, draping her legs over mine. "No," she said, pulling herself up close to me, "I like it."

87

*　*　*

I would wake at dusk thinking it was dawn, and at
dawn thinking dusk. I became, even more than before,
nocturnal. I was hardly ever sure what was going on, but
whatever it was, it was somehow grand.

I walked into the café around one, finally finished with
my studies, and the whole place was empty.

"Hey," I said.

"Hey," somebody said, and she rose up from behind
the counter and tweaked my nose, which seemed to crack
and break, by the sound of it, in twelve different places.
What had she done? I tweaked it, my nose, and it seemed
fine. Then she tweaked her own nose and it broke in
eight or ten places. It was a horrible snapping noise, her
breaking her very own nose like that, between her thumb
and index finger. I reached over and tweaked it, her
nose, and she didn't scream.

"What gives?" I said.

And she reached underneath the counter and brought
out a piece of uncooked spaghetti, put a piece between
her teeth. She shook my hand and broke every bone in it.

"Gimme some," I said, grinning. "This is gonna be
great. Gimme some." And she did and I put a piece between my molars, bent my ear over and bit hard, and my
ear snapped like a twig under a thief's foot. I'd busted my
own ear, but it flapped back. Mary was grinning like her
message board.

"I discovered it," she said.

"You're a' absolute genius," I said.

"Thank you."

"It's okay," I said. "Gimme a handful. I'm going to the
library and look for books on the bottom shelf. My
knees'll pop like rifle shots."

"I've broken seven customers' noses already."

"You're a lover," I said.

"I'm awfully fond of you too."

88

*   *   *

"To believe in Big Red, to believe that what is true for you in your private heart is true for all men—that is genius." And I raised my glass in a mock toast.

"Well," Ford said, "I say he's in love."

"You say, he say, we say, what does it matter in the end? Tell me that," Moto said.

I was watching the little bubbles clinging to the side of my glass. It was fascinating. And there one would go, flinging itself to the surface and the vast ocean of air above. Yaa!

"Is she a Christian, Hart?" Rank asked.

I don't think I heard him. I stuck my finger in the Big Red and pried some of the bubbles from the side of the glass. Yaaaaaa!!

"He's in love," Ford said again. "He looks like Rank. He's got that same expression."

"Maybe it's only in moderation," Moto said. "Maybe it's not for us to know."

"I've got a suggestion," Rank broke in.

"For God's sake, let us in on it, man," Ford said.

"He must have it!" Moto said.

Rank said, "Why don't we ask Hart if he's in love?"

Yaaaaaaaaaaaa!!!

"In front of us all the time!" Ford said.

"I cannot speak," said Moto.

"An uncommon brilliance." That was Ford.

And Moto, "But how should we presume?" He'd read "Prufrock" in freshman English the day before.

Ford started moaning an Everly Brothers tune: "Till I Kissed Her." Rank even tried to get in time with an "oh yeah" or two.

And then Moto said, "Hey, something smells like puppy breath," and he frowned. And then we all got quiet and sniffed the air.

"God."

"Gross."

"Who did that?"

"Somebody's sick."

We all danced out of the room.

"I want some doughnuts," I said. It was twelve forty-five and I'd just gotten back from walking Mary to work.

"Doughnut Run!" Ford screamed, and Moto ventured back into the room for the keys to the hearse.

We marched down the hall banging on each door and hollering, "Doughnut Run," and our numbers swelled to fourteen by the time we rolled through the kitchen and living room downstairs and finally piled in the hearse. We descended on that late-night doughnut shop like a band of doughnut-shop saviors. We bought the old lady out so she could go home early and I thought she was going to cry she was so happy. I put a piece of spaghetti in my mouth and broke my nose for her, to bring her out of it.

"You send me, darling," I said, backing out of the door, clamping onto a doughnut.

"He's in love," Moto said, as we got back in the car.

"I told you," Ford said, "I could tell it a mile away."

"I wish I were a fish," I said, and heaved myself up beside her on the rim of the pool.

"You almost are. Doesn't it hurt your lungs to stay under that long? I mean, don't you just want to explode?" Water dripped off the end of Mary's nose back into the pool.

"You do it for so long and it doesn't hurt anymore. You get used to it. I don't know if you get stronger and the pain goes away, or if you just get used to the pain."

I jumped back in the pool and swam a lap, down to the far end of the pool and back, aiming, on the way back, for Mary's dangling feet. I surfaced in front of her and picked up one of her ankles. We were in the shallow end, only four feet deep, so I could stand up. I picked up her foot by the heel and held it up for inspection. I looked at her ankle on both sides and on top, where there was still

90

a tiny incision scar from an operation when she was a kid. I rubbed my finger over it, and around her ankle, and finally let her foot drop back down into the water. And then I looked over the other ankle, and saw its little scar too.

"How much do they hurt?" I asked.

"They don't hurt at all when you hold them like that."

"No," I said, "how much do they hurt?"

"They hurt a little. They creak and groan and get sore if I let them. If I don't move around some."

"Do you want me to carry you everywhere? I will."

"You goose." And she put her foot on my chest and shoved me backward in the water.

I waded back to her and put my elbows on the edge of the pool just outside each of her knees. I put my fists underneath my chin. She was wearing a blue one-piece bathing suit that was cut low in the back and had a single strap that curved around behind her neck and held the suit up in front. It was a very shiny, tight blue suit. Her skin, where there wasn't any of the light freckles, was the color of a full moon, pale and bright. You could see the faint blue of her blood beneath the skin of her breast-bone. The gold note still dangled from its chain. I reached up and turned it over and over between my fingers, then let it twirl about till it was still again.

I looked up at her. Her face was dry now but her hair was still wet, the red in it glinting. I reached up again, put my finger lightly on the face of the golden note and pushed it slowly back toward her breast, till it came flatly against her, where the patch of freckles left off and the pale skin began. I looked at her and said, "Can I kiss you there? I want to kiss you there."

She said, "Hart!" and looked at me for a long moment and then around the Coliseum. She nodded slowly, her eyes wide open.

I leaned forward, one hand on her sleek side, using the other hand to push the note away an inch or two, and kissed her. She shivered. Then I reached up and put my hand behind her neck, in her damp hair, and leaned her forward so I could kiss her, once on the mouth, and then once, turning her face, behind her ear. She sat back up straight.

"God," she said, "let's get out of here." And she got up and held her hand out to me.

I said, "Go on, I'll meet you after you change," and I swam to the opposite side of the pool, toward the men's locker. But before I could get out of the pool, I had to stick my hand down in my trunks and rearrange myself. I was an absolute show.

In the vast crowd of Sociology class Moto told us that he and Virginia had decided not to see each other again. He said he would never look at another girl as long as he lived. Ford and I offered condolences, but tried to keep it quiet so the professor wouldn't hear and drag us, all three, to the front of the room. Moto just said, "No, no, I just need a faithful Indian companion."

"I do not like them, Sam I am. I do not like green eggs and ham," I said.

"Would you, could you, eat them through a hose? Would you, could you, suck them up your nose?" she asked.

"I would not, could not, eat them with a hose. I would not, could not, suck them up my nose. I do not like them, Sam I am. I do not like green eggs and ham."

"Would you, could you, with Thoreau? Would you, could you, with Othello?"

"I would not, could not, with Thoreau, Othello, Romeo, or even Oz's Scarecrow. Oh me, oh my, oh, when will you let this green eggs and ham thing go?"

"Lions and tigers and bears, oh my," she went on, "lions and tigers and bears, oh my!"

"Roowwrr!" Moto threw out from the back of the

hearse. It was an hour-long trip from school to Grandpa's, and the four of us, Ford, Moto, Mary, and I, were going down to help bale hay. "C'mon, c'mon," he harrumphed, lifting his skinny dukes to Ford, "fight ya with one hand tied behind my back. Oh! Trying to pull an ax on me, eh?"

Mary leaned over and whispered in my ear, "I saw something nasty in the woodshed."

"The horror, the horror."

"The king of beasts, that's me," Moto rolled on.

"And Toto, too?"

"Toto, too."

"There's no place like home." It was all a dream. We were still and the world moved beneath the wheels of the hearse.

Moto looked out the window and asked, "Hey, doesn't the red fern grow around here somewhere?"

"Lord, I cried when I read that book. Big tears rolled out of my eyes," Mary said.

"Felix the cat,"—this was Ford—"the wonderful, wonderful cat, you'll laugh so much your sides will ache, your heart will go pitter-pat, watching Felix, the wonderful cat."

"I remember that," I said. "He had a bag of tricks."

"Davy," Mary said, in as low a voice as she could muster, "Davy, you better not do that; we promised old Mr. Baxter we'd help him prune his peach tree today, Davy. Ruff, ruff."

And Moto took it all in. "He won't care, Goliath. Besides, think of how much fun we'll have at the ball game."

"I don't know, Davy."

And Ford again: "Silver and gold, silver and gold, everyone loves silver and gold. Silver and gold decorations, on every Christmas tree."

"Well, sir, I want to be a Den-Tist."

"What? You're an elf and you'll remain an elf. Now make some choo-choos and smile."

"Ha! Didn't you know? Bumbles bounce!"

"But Rocky, what if Boris and Natasha steal the gold while we're gone?"

"Don't worry, Bullwinkle, I've got it all figured out."

"Dudley Doright, by your side, Inspector, to do my duty to you."

"George, George, George of the jungle, friend to you and me."

"Go, Speed Racer, go, Speed Racer, go, Speed Racer, go!"

"Geo for geo, logy for logy, geology."

"Felix, watch out, it's the evil Master Cylinder."

"Poindexter!"

"A Slinky, a Slinky, it's fun for girls and boys, fun for girls and boys."

"Did you ever have any Silly Putty when you were a kid?" I said.

"Copied every Snoopy cartoon I could lay my hands on," she said.

We drove down the Bluegrass toward Decatur, but I didn't see it from the inside of the hearse out. I was up above and in front of the car, looking through the windshield at Mary in the front seat, and Ford and Moto in back, and me driving, all of us in a row, a group photo, on the way to my grandfather's house in the woods.

"Look," I said, whispering to her, "let's form a rock duo and call ourselves 'There's Stuff on Your Face.' When we're introduced, everyone in the audience will wipe their mug."

"Good," she said, "good, and when we're a success, we'll introduce and endorse a line of Velcro dentures."

"What about a frozen food company? We'll call our chicken fingers 'chicken digits.' What about that?"

"Yes, yes," she whispered, and kissed me on the temple. "Hush."

"Hush?"

"Yes, hush."

She reached up over me and turned off her desk lamp, the only light in the room except for the red dot on the stereo. She had on some classical thing, real soft and slipping.

"Hart, I don't want to go to work tomorrow." By tomorrow she meant twelve in the morning, just another five hours.

"Don't go. I'll call for you."

"I've got to. There's no one else."

"Okay, go."

"Okay."

We were on her bed, which doubled as a couch during the day. She was quiet after that, curled up against me, and I cradled her there. I'd have to leave in a little while, maybe after the record was finished, so she could get some sleep.

In the meantime I let her lie there. I reached up and rubbed my bruised lips, bruised and tender from the kissing that afternoon. I thought that this must be something that passed, or there would be more medical reports on it. A lifetime of swelling lips? The venetian blinds on the little bay window at the end of the room were open, and the light from dusk came in by bars. The whole room was layered. The stereo was in shadow, and the little red light shone brightly, but the record itself swirled through the evening, its edge brisk and aglow. I watched it turn without seeing it turn, knowing it was turning. I heard the music coming out. It hung with the faint bars of light. Mary moved in my arms. There were lights in the distance, yellow and white. They came on one and two at a time and then suddenly a whole string of them, lighting up in series like ideas, on some distant highway. We were way up in the sky. If we'd been here all our lives we'd have called the pattern of lights on the earth constellations and been baffled by their movements. The record fell out with the light, the swinging arm arced with the last faint beam and the machine closed down. The little red light blinked out. It was very quiet. I ran my hand down her jean-covered thigh and back up again. But she didn't move. I felt her even breathing on my arm. She was asleep. She had fallen asleep while I held her. I was stunned It was like a bird lighting on your shoulder, or a mouse deciding to hibernate in your shirt pocket. I don't think I'd ever felt more trusted, so cockily, so chauvinistically, male. She brought her knees up close to us, and I laid my head on her hip, and I, as best I could, watched her sleep.

Rank had been exhorting and dispelling all night, mostly about the crucifixion, and when I finally got to sleep I dreamed. I was sitting at my desk studying and suddenly got up, grabbed the keys and ran out to the hearse. I drove around and around Lexington, looking and looking, trying to hurry, but I kept missing the lights and having to stop. Suddenly Moto and Ford were there in the car with me, and as I looked at them they opened the door. I slammed on the brakes so they wouldn't fall. We were at the foot of a hill, and up on top of the hill were the three crosses, Jesus and the murderer and the thief. We all hurried up the slope and I found Mary, already there. We ran around and around the foot of Christ's cross yelling up at him, yelling and yelling. We yelled and we yelled, moving beneath him, yelling, "Hang on, hang on."

She came from the curtains in her white Grecian evening gown, folds of white cloth, bare shoulders and arms and a slit up one leg, like water over rocks. The black piano stood on the far side of the stage, antithesis, pregnant. She paused before it, placed her rose in the vase on the piano as the others had done, and sat down. I tensed in my chair, loosened my tie. Board up your windows, I thought. Lay in supplies. Something is loosed upon the world. Her hair was down and pulled back behind her ear on one side again, and the tiny diamond flashed at the audience. This was what she'd been practicing for, her creative recital. Four other students had gone before her and she was the last on the program. She tilted the mike down toward her, told us her name, and said, "This is for Hart." No one turned his head toward me. They were all looking at her. She was a pillar. She pushed the mike back up and away, and folded her hands in her lap for a moment. You could have heard a fly's thought. She lifted her arm, the one arm and hand, and began.

And from the start, since I had heard it all before, I was merely alluvial material, so much debris on the bottom of the sea. The currents bumped me along from reef to reef, and a crab scuttled across my chest. I looked up for the barnacled hulls of boats and the feet of birds. The pressure was so intense. I felt myself giving in, disintegrating, becoming grain among grain, a layer of life-born rock. A thin fish puckered at my cheek. My arm caught between two rocks as I was buffeted along by the wind of currents, and I held there. A porpoise put his snout under my other arm and tried to help me along. But it was no use. What could he do? We both cried into the sea. I lay there, looking up, and spoiled, folded in upon myself, flesh giving way, and my bones finally fell free of the rocks and were scattered among crevices and along the ocean floor. I sighed. I was as low down as I could be. There was nothing left for me to do but ascend. Please.

Mary brought her hands away from the keys and I turned to the audience and could tell it was the first time they'd heard her. They were quiet, still gasping for air, though I knew it was useless. They began to clap and while they clapped I understood that Mary was not mine. I'd never met her. She was theirs while they clapped. I thought, I'll never let her play again. She bowed her head and walked back across the stage.

I met her in the foyer of the theater. There was a small reception. All five students were there and some teachers were passing out cider. She couldn't talk to me for the others around her, and so I took my cider and leaned against a wall and watched. I saw her glance at me once during her conversations, she glanced for an aching second or two, but didn't smile.

It was late when we finally left the theater. I gave her my arm and she took it and I could tell she was blinded with talking. So I didn't say anything either, and just cradled her arm. There was no moon, and although it was clear it was still very dark. We walked beneath trees back toward her room.

We walked, and it was like being out on a calm sea, a placid sea, and leaning out over the boat's stern to look at the detached sea. And then suddenly to have a bubble wobble boisterously up from the bottom to the surface and burst in your face. Something was down there, moving around, breathing.

"Hart," she says to me, and Lord, she is still saying this to me, yet, now, still, saying, "Hart, when do we learn how to make love?"

11

I T IS COMING into the heat of the arc, and so after lunch I open the window in my room again, pick up a book and go out to the front porch. Zeke loafs around from the side porch when he hears the door close, and he collapses, a heap of old dog, under the swing I lie in. Some days I'll be out on the farm for a good sixteen hours, but today there's little to do. The wind has fallen off and will only turn a leaf pale side up momentarily. And although it is warm, it is still spring; with spring it's morning all day long.

And so I read, that phenomenon of searching for and accepting clues from complete strangers on our own front porch. It's an invitation I can make to another human without having to suffer his appetite and bad breath, his physical bearing. I can read in my underwear and not feel the least bit embarrassed. I can have bad breath too. I can say, "Oh sure," and "Bullshit," instinctively, and not feel obliged to back it up. I point out fallacies and untruths. I laugh haughtily in their faces. I read like a hero.

> Above the fresh ruffles of the surf
> Bright-striped urchins flay each other with sand.

I've been reading some Hart Crane. My father regularly packages up a box of his books and ships them to me. And this last lot held his own copy of Crane's poems, the one his father bought for him on the day Dad was born. My father never really much cared for it. The spine is still intact. You have to break a book's back to show it any affection at all. There was a short paperback biography in the box too. And I read about Crane folding his coat over the ship's railing at noon and jumping into the sea off the stern. About his feelings for his folks and his trouble with drinking, his ravings and throwings, his homosexuality.

> They have contrived a conquest for shell shucks,
> And their fingers crumble fragments of baked weed
> Gaily digging and scattering.

It was, I think, thrust upon my father like a religion, and although he studied and read, it never overcame him the way his father thought it should. And so when I was born I was named Hart, too, but after my father. He says it's so, as much as I.

> And in answer to their treble interjections
> The sun beats lightning on the waves,
> The waves fold thunder on the sand;

It all had a profound effect upon my dad. He would never push anyone into anything. He wouldn't let my mom send me to church until I was old enough "to decide on my own." And so he doesn't send me his copy of Crane till I'm twenty-three. I remember taking the book out of the box and recognizing it immediately, wondering if Dad sent it to me for my sake or for his dad's.

I read the paperback biography, more of a pamphlet than a paperback, more of a résumé than a biography, first, before the book. Crane's father was nothing like mine.

> And could they hear me I would tell them:
> O brilliant kids, frisk with your dog,
> Fondle your shells and sticks, bleached
> By time and the elements;

Zeke groans under me and stretches his front legs out, draws them back, and again closes his eyes. He cares nothing for poetry. I reach down and rub his back.

He killed himself with a great deal of poetic justice, Crane did. His poetry soaks with the ocean, laves in it. His lovers were often sailors. He was born of the womb and felt a returning. A beautiful death. Hemingway's suicide was just as poetic: At one time he was fond of blasting the faces off hyenas for their looks, and ended up placing a shotgun to his brow and doing the same; just as poetic, yet never sentimentalized because someone had to deal with the blood on the walls. Crane. He should have, at the least, washed up on the beach, bone and shirt.

               but there is a line
You must not cross nor ever trust beyond it
Spry cordage of your bodies to caresses
Too lichen-faithful from too wide a breast.

I read, and am pulled inexorably into the tragedy. I
may be a hero, but I have no will of my own. I am caught
in the undertow.

               The bottom of the sea is cruel.

But that does not mean I do not flail at the water.
I have thought of that too, his final answer, the boiling
wake, the white water turning calm and blue. No one
having to bother with my bones. But the desire for it is
not there. The fear of it is gone, it's true, but there is no
desire either. The idea doesn't hold water. They're beginning to use umbilical cords to replace diseased arteries.
It's possible to begin again.
No desire, but I understand. To tell, we must first be
lost in fatal tides. One has to sink to appreciate the neces-
sity of swimming. Even if existence has no meaning, it
doesn't mean that existence itself is unworthy. But people
don't kill themselves because life has no meaning, but because it has so much, sometimes simply too much.
Gertrude Vogt, a friend of Crane's, was on the boat
that day, in the warm water north of Havana. Hart came
up from belowdecks at noon, badly beaten by the sailors
the night before. He was thirty-three. He folded his coat
over the railing, like he'd come back for it, and jumped.
"Just once I saw Crane," she said, "just once I saw Crane,
swimming strongly, but never again."
This is the lifesaver I hold in my hand for a moment
and then throw to him: that he is still out there swimming.

12

SINKING in our own sweat down into one another, all the night made we our bed to swim. Arroyo before, but she coursed through me, made us brimming, and brimming overflow, abundant. We were more. In her room we bathed, melted down, became liquid, flow. We were conceived, were wrought in each other's hands, her thigh forming under my moving palm, my lips molded to her breast. "Come on," we said, "come on, now."

She sat on her bed with her hands folded and pressed tightly between her knees, while I unbuttoned her blouse, button by slow button, my eyes fixed intently on each button as I worked. Her hair fell on both sides of my face, loose and curled, ardently her odor, and I pressed up through it and found her mouth. She rolled back over onto the bed on her back and I crawled up and sat on her thighs, unbuttoned the last white button and pulled at the part of the shirt tucked in her jeans, freed it from the front and she lifted up, arched, so I could pull it out underneath. It came loose and I put my hands inside her shirt and under her shoulder blades, pivoted her up toward me. Clothes were such filthy bargains. They were always out of fashion. She stuck her arms up in the sky like a sleepy kid and I dragged her shirt off and dropped it off the edge of the bed. I reached around and fumbled with her bra snap while she pressed her nose into my chest.

"Here," she said, "let me show you." And she reached around back and with a deft twist unsnapped the hooks.

"It's like a damned puzzle," I said. "Some awful prude designed that snap."

And she lay back down and I leaned forward and with both hands slid the straps off her shoulders and then the cups away from her, and let that drop off the bed too. She was so white. The blue of her veins was even clearer on her breasts, under the clear white skin, like some gorgeous secret. I held tightly to the rope of her ribcage while she reached up and opened my shirt, each button a bit quicker than the last, and then pulled the hem out of my pants. I unbuttoned the cuffs myself and took the shirt off.

And she said, "Let me," and I gave her the wadded-up shirt so she could drop it off the edge of the bed to the floor.

Even though it wasn't cold I shivered, and she reached up again to rub down the goose pimples on my arms. I sat back farther on her legs and popped open the top button on her jeans, and then the next, and I could already see the elastic and lace of her underwear, and then the next button, and realized how much I truly hated button-up jeans, and then the next, and next buttons, and finally finished, turning back one flap, and there the hollow between her thigh and abdomen, the dark patch of her hair under the panties. The hair came up in a faint line to her navel and stopped there.

She lifted up again and pushed me back over, sat on my thighs, and popped the button on my jeans. I had been hard, it seemed, for hours, and when she slid the zipper back toward her I slipped forward, raising the fabric of my shorts, able, at last, to breathe. She folded the flaps back and then inched back on the bed, her breasts hanging down, perfect, and then put her thumbs inside my pant legs, underneath my heels, and pulled. I lifted up with her second pull and the jeans came off. I was more embarrassed that my socks were revealed than my underwear. They were dark blue and looked funny down there alone. Then, standing on her knees, she put her thumbs inside the hips of her pants and sort of shimmied them down, sat on the edge of the bed to pull them the rest of the way off. I took off my socks and kneeled on the floor before her. She still sat on the bed but had her back to the wall. Her feet dangled off the edge. I pulled off her short white socks, and held her foot in my hand, kissed its small scar, and the bottom of each of her toes. I kissed her around her lousy ankles and up the back of her calf, and behind her knee, up the inside of her smooth thigh and nuzzled her silk. I slid my hands under her rear and latched on to the elastic there and dragged her underwear out from under and then off. She lifted one leg to help me. I was standing by then and she leaned forward and pulled the front of my shorts out and then down, down to my ankles, and I stepped out of them.

She spread herself out on her back and said, "Come on," and so I gingerly climbed over one of her legs and stood on my knees between her thighs, facing her. "Come on," she said, raising up and pulling me down. And, pulling me, she fell back on her pillow, her hair flowing, and I finally, falling, met her body. I have never touched anything so alive as her skin. It was hard and enveloping, and I breathed against her. I wanted to eat her whole. We moved against each other, mouth to mouth, and I ground my groin into her thick dark hair, rubbing. I could not hold her close enough to me; I used all of my strength and weight to suck her in and nothing was enough. I wanted to breathe and drink her.

I pulled away from kissing her and unclasped the note around her neck, let it drop to the rug. And fell back to her throat and the soft place behind her ear, and she rocked. I put my palms in the sheets, against the mattress, and pushed myself down. I bit and sucked along the crest of her freckled shoulders, down the muscle of

104

her arm, kissed the sweaty palms of her hand. I moved back up to her breastbone and then scraped the stubble of my chin down the flat hollow between her breasts and she arched her back. I grabbed her with both hands at the hips, rocked them slowly, and then fell slowly myself to her ashen chest. I ran my mouth and tongue under the soft bulbous underside of her breasts, and then up on top and around to the dark circle of her nipples, hard and tender, like nothing else. I batted them over and over with my tongue like gum and she enjoyed it. Then along her ribs, back and forth like a staircase down, across her flat belly, where I tugged gently at the hair around her navel with my teeth, and to the place where her legs joined her abdomen, that crease, hollow where I rested my cheek. She raised my head again and again on the wave of her breathing.

Nuzzled again the hair of her groin, and slid back, moving to the side her moist thighs. She was thick and heady, and with my hands I parted her hair. She moved. She folded in and in upon herself, and out to me, and I ran my tongue through her, along each fold and tuck, till I stopped where she held me, and then I waited, working, for her to become pointed and hard, till she ebbed and rocked in my arms and fell out, flung her hands into my hair and pulled me back up, where I could hardly hold on for her breathing, shuddering, sinking and rising. But she held me in her arms and wrapped her slick legs around me, and I was bound.

She kissed me and rolled me over on my back, unfolded. She lifted up from me and held herself over me, stood on her knees, straddling my hips, and then took me in her hands. She held me up, erect, so she could slide down over me. I wanted to throw my hips to the moon. She sat there around me, arched her back and reached up with both hands pulling her hair back behind her head and then let it fall. She was going to play me. I put my hands on the juncture of her hips and held on. She

105

rocked back and forth till I finally had to let go, sliding up through her and falling out, soaking and slick; I let go and held her down to my chest so she wouldn't go on.

"Okay," I said, "okay."

She held me tight, while I shivered, broke up, and breathed. She lay on my chest quietly, holding me. I have watched a sculptor carve marble into cloth, and I've seen a hugely obese old woman pull herself up into a bus, one step at a time. It was all the same. Lord, such variety. I put my left hand behind her head and with my right embraced her.

"I love you."

"I love you, too."

"Let's not ever get up from here. It's just May; we can get up in September, when school starts again."

"Okay."

"Don't go away this summer."

"I'll come back. Promise."

"My sweet Mary."

And she said, "You bet."

She rolled off me, and I was nothing compared to what I had been. I was more. She loved me. She lay beside me, my dear love, my awesome lousy-ankled love, and I rolled over too, moved my face slowly down along her, rubbing my nose and brow between her breasts and smelling, my cheek against the brown down of her abdomen, and stopping at her hollow navel, pausing to place my ear over her cockleshell navel, and listening for the ocean there.

13

I ROLL out of the porch swing among creaking chains and carry the book back to my room, put it on the brick-and-board shelf with the others. The wind has scattered my papers on the floor again, and so this time, after I gather them up and stack them, I take a brick from the bookshelf and pin them to my desktop. There, I think. I am something. Then I pick up my field desk and carry it back out to the porch. The field desk is this thing I bought at an auction, an old oak military field desk that officers used while on maneuvers. It's sort of a briefcase on legs that, with the push of a button, unfolds like a miracle into a complete office: letter bins, pencil trays, blotter, files, et cetera. I feel like a cartoon when I push the button. I use it mostly to write letters from. The big desk in my room seems awfully forbidding to a simple letter. I set the field desk in front of the swing and sit down, nudging Zeke out from under so I'll have a place to put my feet. He gets up and sniffs the desk, making sure I don't have a candy bar up there or something, and then pirouettes again and groans to another halt and slumber behind the desk.

Dear Mom and Dad,

Got your package in the mail day before yesterday. Thanks. I ate two of the candy eggs and gave one to Zeke. I'm sure he appreciated it too. He kept looking at my magical hands for more. Dad, please tell Pap I've been reading the

107

Crane stuff you sent and really like it. Most of it's beyond me but I'm working on it. Please remember to tell him. Everything is going well here. Zeke is healthy, jumped a rabbit this morning but didn't catch it as usual. That horse I'm taking care of is getting a little less shy. The cows are all well too—they send their moos. I'm going to town this evening to pick up a salt block for them, for the summer.

That's all for now. The mailman should be around soon and I want to get this down to the box, and I've got an idea you'll call tonight anyway. If you see Moto around, tell him to give me a call.

Love,
Hart

I fold the paper, stick it in an envelope, stamp it, and walk down the rocky driveway to the mailbox down the road. Zeke follows me. He understands most of my wanderings, their purpose—to feed cows, or to fix a fence—but this trip down to the mailbox every day baffles him. I pull down the little tin door and pop in my letter, then raise the desperate red flag of our hopes.

I don't think there is any more common expectancy among men than the coming of the mail. I think the post office is the most honorable institution ever institutionalized. It gives and receives seemingly without knowledge of the difference between the two. My postman is the friendliest guy I know. He is my hero. I have never trusted a stranger so completely. The prospects are maddening. There is nothing sadder than a lost letter, words cast into the void. If you didn't have to wear a uniform, I think I'd join up. Carry a letter to my love, bring another back to me. I can hear the shrill squeal of my postman's brakes at the farthest reach of the farm, and I come a-running, and to top the hill and see that mailbox crammed so full the door won't close can just break my heart. What can it be? Who from, bless their heart? For me? It could be from anywhere on earth, a millennium old, just now getting here. It could be an epistle from Paul, or even Judas, a letter from an American farmer, a note from Alexander Pope, or perhaps a general letter of Safe Conduct. I am overwhelmed by the possibilities. A letter, thank God, of acceptance. Any letter breaking the news. Once, during an election year, I received an honest-to-God open letter to the President! And even if it is true that it is most often—that word that coats the tongue with motor oil—a bill, a dun, I am yet to be disillusioned. I cannot neglect the possibility that someone is writing me a letter at this very moment. Sealing it like the secret it is and putting money on it, bribing the postman, to see that it reaches my hands safely.

Zeke and I wait for a truck to pass, then recross the road and head back up the driveway to the house. The trip, to him, has been perfectly useless. He doesn't know what a letter can mean, why we save them for so many years, some for a whole lifetime.

There is a box in Grandpa's old study, and another in Grandmother's sewing room. Both are full of old letters. I don't know what to do with them, other than knowing that I'll never throw them away. They will be kept for at least two lifetimes, mine and theirs. The box in the study is filled with letters to Grandpa from her, and the box in the sewing room, letters from him to her. They are small boxes, maybe only fifty letters in each. They were never apart for long. They're mostly from the war, written on fragile paper, hers in ink and his in pencil. Hers are all postmarked Decatur, and his London, Paris, Genoa, and others. I put the two boxes together when I first found them, ordered all the letters chronologically, and then read them straight through. Often they'd write two letters to each other before receiving an answer to the first. They're all long letters. All brittle and young and soiled and aching. I read them and thought my story was as old as the hills. She said she was waiting for him and he said, "Honey, I've killed a man," and she said, "I'm still waiting." There are pictures in the envelopes too, and pieces of maps, ticket stubs, crude drawings of buildings and an occasional postcard, even a few pressed flowers he took from a field, can you believe it, in France, sixty-four years ago. All of it sent across the ocean in the hull of a ship.

And then there were a few more letters in Grandpa's box that weren't from her. They were from my mom, after she'd just married Dad and moved to Texas. I didn't read those. I didn't find any letters from Mom in Grandma's box. Mom, I guess, had never been away from home while Grandma was alive. Grandma died when Mom was ten.

I read their letters, then separated them and put them back where they belonged. I have my letters too, and will always want them where they belong. They're all from Mary, from the summer of that year, when she went home to Colorado. I keep them in a shoe box on the top shelf of my closet. I've read them once or twice since then, but nothing ever seems to change when I do, so for the last couple of years I've let them lie. Sometimes, I think, if there were a fire that shoe box wouldn't protect them, and I'd lose them, but that doesn't seem to be the most important thing anymore. They were, like all things, written in water. And besides, it is my memory that counts.

As I fold up the field desk and carry it back to my room, I hear the squeal of the postman's brakes and my heart leaps up. I walk to the door, and it's true, the flag is down, the flag is down, and Zeke and I start out for the mailbox, I crammed with curiosity and he shaking his head, thinking, Lord, here we go again.

14

PIANO MUSIC played all summer long; we worked and ate and bathed in its playing; it seemed the wind blew to the music of a piano. The cows mooed and the sun glowed, and Zeke, from that summer on, displayed a natural grace, matured into a dog that would let a bird perch on his paw. All the day was dusk, syncopation, and we moved through it stealthily, as if in slow motion, but always, aware. And the piano music played, never missing, missed.

Morning and memory gone, barely conscious, face pressed in pillow, I'd reach over and plug a cassette into the stereo and Mary's music would fill the old house. I'd grin into my pillow. Moto would scream from his room down the hall, "Aaaaannh! Morning! AGAIN!" And we would all begin the summer again. Grandpa was forever startled to wake up and meet someone in the hall. It would make his day.

The semester had ended in one great whirlpool of people and events. There was a calm before the swirl, when I spent every free hour in Mary's room, when I'd listen to her play, and school was its daily bother. But then we all trembled, as if we were about to boil, and then the bottom fell out. The pledges' final stage of initiation, Hell Week, and our finals, and the packings and leavings of everyone we'd lived with for the past nine months became a sort of vortex where we flailed for handholds. Our first year of college was over, and while Moto and I had done well, Ford had just been knocked around. He talked about not coming back. Wyeth left for the summer to work in some kind of carcinogenic chemical plant in Cloverport, and Rank was enrolled in a three-month seminary down on the Tennessee border, in the Cumberlands. Moto and Ford and I left to work for Grandpa in Decatur. He didn't need us but he could use us, and I would have felt funny going home to Texas for the summer anyway. I'd always spent my summers with him. We decided to save our trip home till the end of the summer.

Mary and I spent the last thirty-three hours before her flight to Colorado in her room. She let me have all of her practice tapes, tapes she'd recorded of herself to listen to later. I bought a cassette player the day she left. She quit The Pancake & Egg Place but they told her they'd hire her back in September if she wanted. The last time she walked out of there she took eight or ten huge breaths. "To get that place out of me." She even had me bring her jeans so she could change out of her brown-and-orange uniform before she left, so she wouldn't have to come back to turn it in. "At the very least," she said, grinning, "I won't cook an egg for another three months." Mary had done well in school too. Better than that, really. She got all kinds of awards for her playing, and an extra scholarship.

I put her on the plane out at Bluegrass Field and after the thirty-three hours, I said, "I'm sorry."

And she said, "No, that's silly, I can sleep on the plane. But I'm sore all over."

"Me too. Ain't it great?"

"You'll write me all the time."

"All the time."

And we hugged and she walked down the corridor to the plane. I watched it taxi off. I said to myself, "God, three months," and slumped back down into the hearse, drove my poor body home, and slept for the next sixteen hours.

Moto woke, startled at his own existence, and screamed, and we all began the day. Grandpa descended the stairs like a buffalo, came through my door, then Ford and Moto's, like a pirate boarding a ship, and said, "What! Still in bed!" and then turned toward the kitchen, astounded. He took no prisoners. We straggled into the kitchen in jeans, sneakers, and ragged T-shirts, already depleted and aghast at the thickness of the humid day. Walking was like wading through neck-deep water. Moto hadn't opened his eyes completely yet, and he walked with his arms out and hands spread, hoping to stave off disaster. Ford was just the opposite. He'd splashed his face with water and come into the kitchen like a breakfast cereal box, eyes propped wide, skin pinched, but just as blind as Moto. There was too much light.

"I need some Big Red," he said.

"Get me some," Moto ordered, and grabbed hold of a chair, when he finally found one, as if he'd just recognized it as refuge from a long hard life.

"Boys, boys"—Grandpa beamed—"so much to do today," as he dived into the pots and pans underneath the counter.

"When's Saturday hit this burg?" Ford groaned.

"Ya got no Saturdays this part of the country?" Moto squealed. He was genuinely concerned.

"Did either of you boys ever try to explain Saturday to a weed, or a hungry cow? Can't be done." Give Grandpa credit; he didn't mind sparring with them. He fixed our breakfast while we clutched our glasses of Big Red between both hands. "Can't see how you boys can drink that sugar-water this early in the day. That stuff is harder swallowed than whiskey."

"You get used to it," I said.

"You go without women so long," Ford said.

"You gotta substitute something," Moto said.

Grandpa turned around with our eggs, ladled them out. "Well, I've seen grown men take to it on account of losing their wife or one of their children. It ain't a joking matter."

113

We let the kidding go then, and ate our eggs. Jesus, he could turn on you like that sometimes. Everything had been categorized long ago in his mind, down to the neatest detail, and he'd decided, maybe thirty or forty years earlier, whether he'd ever laugh at a joke about a particular subject—drinking over women, whatever. There were no gray areas in life, as far as he'd seen.

Until it came to farming. Nothing was new enough. He'd accept almost any suggestion, use any hybrid. I think that he thought the earth was some kind of lock, and with the right combination all he had to do was swing open the safe door. But whatever the combination, whatever the correct nitrogen content of the soil, it always had to be accompanied by a constant sweat and vigil. That was just part of the deal with the earth. He always knew the right series of numbers, but the door weighed a ton and swung on rusty hinges. No matter how many people were on the farm on a given day, it always took just that many to swing that door, to get through the hours to dinner.

We ate our breakfast quietly, and after running water over our plates went out the door in front of Grandpa, walking the plank, so to speak. Moto headed toward the garage, where he, mechanical genius that he was, was overhauling the old manure spreader. Ford picked up his hoe, which was leaning next to the door, and trudged off to the dew-struck tobacco. It was his pet project to behead weeds amongst the burley relentlessly. Get them in the morning, he said, before they become acquainted with life. Then he'd make a sadistic chopping motion with his hands, and make that horrible sound, *yee-yee-yee-yee,* from the shower scene in *Psycho.*

I walked alongside Grandpa, pounding my chest. "Just embrace this morning, would you," I said. He had no nose for the fine art of sarcasm. "Yes, sir," I said, "makes you want to bust open like a pea pod." I looked at him again. Still no acknowledgment. I said, "I might just sing."

114

This brought him out of his snoot. He let me close the gate to the barnyard. I opened the barn doors while he got the tractor started. Zeke had caught up to us then, after bothering Moto and Ford till they couldn't stand him any longer. He was soaking wet from chasing something in the dew, and greeted me by dashing up close, spreading his four legs out sawhorse style, and shaking himself dry. I was wrong. It wasn't dew. He'd been in a ditch somewhere. He shook himself again, his body a taut wire plucked. He was still then, each hair standing individually. He looked like he'd been shocked. Grandpa rumbled through with the tractor and I pitched a couple of vitamin blocks on the wagon. Zeke and I pitched ourselves on too, and we were off.

He was a quiet man. I never realized it more than when he was on the tractor. Language was not for him. He would just as soon listen. He didn't like rock music, but the roar of that tractor engine in his ear was bliss.

Moto had bought four or five cassette decks at a junk sale and mounted them to anything that had electricity and would hold still long enough. The hearse had one, one was in the garage, one in the house, and one on the tractor. Grandpa pushed the cassette in and Mary's music followed us over the farm. It was one of her practice tapes, the one where she kept messing up and saying, "Damn." Grandpa liked it best. He turned the volume up as high as it would go and Mozart twinkled all around us, difficult contrapuntal cadenzas raining down on me and Grandpa, as we tractored out to count cows.

He had a big group this time, more than a hundred head, that he'd bought on the speculation that a good deal of them would die. They were all young pregnant heifers, too young to be pregnant. He'd bought them, cheaply, from an inexperienced farmer who was trying to make money off calves too early. The cows needed at least another year before they'd be mature enough to give birth safely, but they were ready now, in the heat of

115

the summer. We checked them often. Almost twenty had calves on the ground already. Only one calf and heifer had died. We were up at all hours pulling calves out of cows, counting to make sure one wasn't off somewhere giving birth, listening for bawling heifers.

I jumped off the wagon to open the gate into the third pasture, and Grandpa drove on through. The cows, spread out over twenty acres, all looked up at us at once, the way the bows of violins in an orchestra will sometimes salute you in the middle of a piece like a chorus line. We drove slowly through them, the tractor idled down and the piano music clear and resolute, counting. Grandpa counted and I counted. Zeke merely made swipes at them with his paw. We came out of them at the bottom of the field and Grandpa said, "One nineteen."

"One nineteen," I said.

Mary stopped playing and said, "Damn."

No new attractions had come in the night. I was disappointed. Every morning seemed to hold some promise, like Christmas. Finding no new cows was like an empty mailbox. Grandpa pulled up next to a galvanized feeder and I put the two mineral blocks in it and he pulled off again. Then we made another round through the herd, checking over the calves, making the heifers that were lying down get up, making sure they could get up. They were all fine, although some of them were so heavy they looked like tugboats. They stood up like they were pushing the earth out from underneath them, their wombs stationary, the center of the universe. They got up and looked at me and Grandpa, would have said, "Okay?" if they could have. We felt terrible for forcing so much unnecessary effort. A few of them wandered sluggishly over to the mineral blocks we'd just dropped off, and the rest, who weren't eating, lay back down. A whole field of cows on the brink, waiting to contract and explode. We looked them over and got out of there.

And then into the next field, where we stopped at

116

Grandpa's one line shack, an outhouse-looking place where he kept spare wire, a few boards and tools. He came out with a hammer and saw, and a coffee can of rusty nails. I picked up a couple of boards leaning against the shack and put them on the wagon. Then we headed off again, for the old footbridge.

The creek that runs around one side of the farm has an island in it. It's a knob that just poked itself up out of the middle of the creek bottom a while back—a few million years ago. It was right in the creek's way, and so the creek had to go around. It decided to go around both ways, I guess, to see which was shorter. On one side the water is shallow and quick, and on the other side, the side facing Grandpa's farm, the water is deep and slow. The island is shaped like a Christmas ornament, tear-dropped. There is an old footbridge across this deep side, built even Grandpa knew not when. He just kept it up.

We pulled up to the little bridge, and Grandpa turned the old Ford off, and turned down the piano music too. It was only water over a spillway then, very soft and smooth over the moss, the music. He took the tools and I carried the two boards down to the creekside. We both walked out on the bridge, over the water, and jumped up and down.

"This board here, and this one," he said.

And I said, "This one, too, and we need a nail in this handrail here." A leaf floated by under us.

He took up the old boards and I laid them on the ones from the shack for sizing, and sawed new slats. Then he took a few nails out of the coffee can, rubbed the rust on his shirt, and hammered the boards in place. I jumped up and down on them. Then I took the hammer from him and nailed down the loose handrail.

"There," he said.

It was a good old bridge, seldom used. We put the tools and old boards back on the wagon, and then I followed him back across the footbridge to the knob. It was land good for only one thing. Perhaps only an acre altogether, it was too rocky and steep, too overgrown with locust and briers, papaw, too hard to get to, for farming. A cow would lose more weight climbing it than she'd gain from its meager grass. I followed him up what looked like a deer trail. He held the head-high branches for me till I passed. He was puffing pretty hard and leaning on tree trunks, so I told him to slow down.

He said, "Yeah. We'll make it."

We climbed all the way to the top of the knob. The briers and small trees were cleared there. The ground was leaf-covered from ranks of big maples and oaks. The graves were in the middle of the trees.

I'd been there before, but every time I returned I was overwhelmed with my history, the weight and range of it, how much I didn't and never would know. We walked to the graves, eleven of them, the stone markers thinner the older they were. They were all scattered in the open beneath the trees, like something growing themselves, cracked and lichen-blotched. If you didn't know they were there, you might walk right through them and never guess you were in a cemetery. One headstone, a great-great-uncle of mine, was half buried in the trunk of a tree. The tree folded around the grave like it was a baby. Grandma's stone was the newest, and it had been there for thirty years. Grandpa bent down next to it and raked away a few leaves. Then he got up, brushed his pants, and began to walk around the hilltop, picking up branches that had fallen in the last storm. I helped him. We threw them over the side of the hill.

We walked back through the grove, and he stopped, folded his arms, and scratched the back of his elbows.

"You see," he said, pointing, "I'll go here, and there's still room for all of us. Your momma and daddy over there, if he wants, and you and whoever you find to go with. All you've got to do is keep out the briers and pick up the windfall." And then he started back down the deer path.

118

"And the bridge," he said, walking over it, "that's got to—"

"Right," I said, interrupting him, a little tired of it.

Zeke and I jumped back up on the wagon and Grandpa drove us back toward the house. Zeke had been swimming. He smelled a little better than he did that morning. He lay there, paws a-front, his tongue lolling. I reached over, pretending I was going to scratch his jowl, but instead I grabbed hold of his big tongue. His eyes narrowed and crossed and he jumped up and pried himself back away from me. Then he stood there, working his tongue back and forth, seeing if it still worked. I rubbed my palm along my jeans.

We dropped the tools off at the shack, chugged back through the cattle, and through the gate, down the hill to the barn. We parked the tractor and were heading for the house when someone in the barn yelled, "You can do it! Fly! Fly!" We looked up at the open loft door and suddenly, out of it, like a fly out of a whale's mouth, came a tiny rubber band–powered balsa airplane. It blitzed over our heads and did a couple of Immelmann loops, ran out of torque and floated, in serene circles, down into the center of the pond. Moto came to the loft door. "No, no!" And then disappeared, till he ran out of the barn door, passed us and dived into the water, scattering the ducks, to rescue his plane. He'd been designing the little contraptions all summer and testing them from the loft door. The paradox was that his best flyers made it all the way out to the pond, and the water ruined them.

Grandpa and I watched him swim out for the plane, make it about halfway before Zeke caught him from behind. Zeke knew the only reason a human got in the water was to have fun. And he was a retriever and so he retrieved Moto. Moto beat him off once and swam after the plane again, but Zeke, head thrust forward, nostrils flaring, furious dog paddle, caught him again. Moto gave up. He turned around and followed Zeke back to shore.

119

He crawled out, next to Zeke, and while Zeke shook water on him, he watched his plane.

He said, "Too late now. It's soaked up enough water to save India. It'd never fly again."

Grandpa patted him on the shoulder. "I thought you were supposed to be working on that spreader, anyway."

"Finished," Moto said. "It's in the side yard." And he tromped off, a downed pilot, back toward the front lines. I thought he might shake his fist at the sky at any moment.

Grandpa said, as we followed Moto, "You fixed her and painted her and everything?"

"Yeah," Moto said.

And we rounded the corner of the garage, and it was true. There the manure spreader sat in the side yard in all her bawdy glory. He'd painted all the working mechanisms, the wheels, levers, and tongue, fire-engine red. And the box itself, which held the manure, was a bright baby pink. Grandpa put his hands in his back pockets and walked around and around it. On one side Moto had painted, in gold, a silhouette of two fingers pinching a nose.

"Well?" Moto asked.

I was ready to kill him at the slightest motion of Grandpa's hand.

Grandpa tested all the mechanisms to see if everything worked, and slapped at the new boards Moto had replaced in the box.

Finally, Grandpa said, "Why did you do this?"

"I didn't think about it," Moto said.

"You're a strange boy, but you do good work."

And that's all there was to it. Sometimes old people will surprise you.

Grandpa said, "After lunch we'll take it over to the barn and clean out the stalls, see how she does."

"Okay," Moto said. He was smiling now, water still dripping off his face.

We started toward the house. Grandpa saw Ford out in the tobacco and yelled, waved him home, and then went inside. Moto and I waited. Ford trudged out of the waist-high tobacco, swinging his hoe. He walked down the dirt road between the tobacco and fence. He walked into the side yard, saw the pink manure spreader.

He said, "He's finally gonna get his, isn't he, Hart?"

I slowly shook my head.

"Why not?"

"Grandpa just let it go. He said he did good work," I said.

The neck of Ford's T-shirt hung down about a foot with the weight of his sweat. The sweat ran off him everywhere. There were big dark rings of dirt on his neck, and dirt in the inside crease of his elbow.

He asked Moto, "Why are you all wet?"

"Been swimming."

"Hart, I'm probably gonna get after him with my hoe here in a minute. You better do something."

I started pushing Moto toward the house. I told Ford, "Go cool off in the pond." And then out of meanness I added, "Take Zeke with you."

"I don't want him saving me every two minutes," Ford said, and he let his hoe tumble over against the house. "Stay," he said, and pointed his finger at Zeke. Zeke looked away, ran his tongue over his face, and then let it hang out. He yanked back and bit at a flea.

Ford headed for the pond. "He'll still try to save me," he said. "I know when I least expect it he'll try to save me."

Grandpa fixed us sandwiches for lunch. Fried bologna. He made about ten of them, stacked them on a plate. We ate them like they were good. We ate them all, and then lounged around out on the front porch, willing to give in to the day, say uncle, anything, to stay out of the sun. I started to lie down in a swing, but only got halfway there before I remembered.

"Anybody get the mail yet?" I said.

"Lord," Ford said, "he guards that mailbox like he was a hangar and it was his baby. I got the mail. You didn't get anything."

"You sure?" I said.

"I retraced my steps twice to make sure I didn't drop anything, and then I called the Postmaster General in Washington. He said you didn't get anything today. He has his hopes up for tomorrow, but sadly reports nothing today. I'm sure."

Moto giggled. Grandpa ran his hand over his face and squeezed at the corners of his mouth.

"Big hilarious occasion," I said. I was really pissed. I hadn't gotten any mail.

"Well," Grandpa said, slapping his knees, "now that the mail's come, let's go shovel some manure and see what kind of mechanic Moto here is." He got up, stepped off the porch, and we followed him, as listless as a new idea that's just failed. We all came out from underneath the shade of the maples in front of the house, looked up at the sun, and sneezed.

"Who made this country?" Moto said. "I always feel like I'm walking through a clothesline of sheets just out of the washer."

"Don't cuss the water, boys," Grandpa hushed. "It's why we got such a pretty green country and can feed more than one cow to a hundred acres." A reference to our home state.

"Yeah?" Ford said. "Well, you see here, all this rain, it kills your several various different kinds of plants they grow in Texas there. You gotta have dry country."

"Yeah," Moto added, "it's okay if you care for green. What about your earth tones? There's some beauty for you."

Grandpa handed pitchforks down out of the tack room to us, pointed at the stalls, and then left to hook the tractor to the spreader.

122

"Your basic earth tones," I said, gesturing toward the manure.

And Ford said, "You know, I sure miss school." Something Moto and I thought we'd never hear.

We turned a couple of cows and calves out into the barnyard and then each of us took a stall, pitching the manure out the door into the breezeway. After five or ten minutes Moto said, "Hey, something smells bad." His senses processed information at a blinding rate. Grandpa backed the spreader into the breezeway, and after we'd raked the stalls down to earth, we pitched the manure up into the box of the spreader. Most of the dung was dry and loose, but some recent accretions had to be handled carefully. You just sort of ladled them like a pizza up into the box. When we'd dragged the breezeway clean, I climbed up into the loft and threw down a couple of bales of straw. We spread this in the stalls. And as Grandpa pulled the spreader up into the first pasture, we ushered the calves and cows back into their rooms. We put the pitchforks up, after some sparring, and walked back up to the house.

Grandpa had made it through the gate into the field now, and we all stood and watched him. He set the power takeoff in motion and the big teeth on the back of the spreader began to turn, and the conveyor boards in the bottom of the box brought the manure back to the teeth. A working manure spreader is something to see. It's designed to cover a wide swath of pasture at one pass, and do it quickly. It's no fun to be out there when the air is full of manure spores. The teeth finally bit into the manure and a great green arc of manure spread against the sky. It was a fine, even spray, like a casting of rice at a wedding. It arced outward from the back end of the pink spreader like a rainbow.

Ford said, "Boy, I'd give anything to be able to dump like that."

"That's disgusting," I said.

"It works," Moto said, "I fixed it. It was broke and I fixed it."

I watched the old man drive his tractor. He leaned forward, his hands on top of the wheel and his forearms resting below. He turned occasionally to check on the spreader, and as he pulled his body back around, he'd spit out a stream of tobacco juice over the fender of the big wheel. He was a tiny brown man on a red-and-gray tractor pulling a pink manure spreader far up in a green field. The world was full of color and action, of anticipation.

He finished after a while. He drove down into the side yard and we washed out the box of the spreader. Moto was very proud.

Grandpa said, "That's enough for today, boys." And I thought that's it, it's come evening and I am one day closer to Mary's homecoming, her Hartcoming. My heart went *pink-pink-punk-pink*. And Grandpa and I and Ford went into the house to wash our hands. We all stood at the sink, holding our hands out, waiting turn. Then Ford nudged me, and nodded at the window. Grandpa was looking now too. Moto was out in the yard, scratching his head, trying to get rainwater out of an old tire.

Grandpa said, "Here, boys," and gave us the soap, and we all washed our hands under the running water. Moto came in then, and we all looked up from our hands, and recognized him as one of our own. He paused, worried.

"What's going to happen?" he said. "What's going to happen?"

15

I CARRY the mail back up to the house at arm's length. It's just a bill and a giveaway. Zeke sometimes has the right attitude about the whole affair. I crawl back into the swing, Zeke bellies in under me, and I try to make the most of what's come. The bill is a water bill, only a few dollars: a bargain for all the water Zeke and I can drink in a month, hundreds of gallons, a glassful at a time. I look at the bill again. Hundreds of gallons? We better go easy on that stuff. It hasn't rained in a day or two. And the giveaway, a chance to win a million dollars from a clearance house, just a slim chance, yes, but greater than the one that got me born, so I'll take the odds and send off the enclosed card. They say I don't have to buy anything to win. So it is not such a bad day's haul, the mail. And anyway, it will come again tomorrow. This was just a day's deliverance.

Beneath me, Zeke is already fast asleep. He falls asleep easily, leading a dog's life, and dreams his safari dreams. His feet tremble and race against the open air. He can catch a rabbit lying down. But I've heard him whimper too and, aye, there's the rub.

I yawn, and remember how Moto used to yawn through his nose. He had yawned once in a class, mouth wide, like he was waiting on a train, and the professor had made him get up and go home to bed. So he'd perfected this yawning-through-the-nose technique. It took him a semester to do it. He would feel a yawn coming on and brace himself, fighting to keep his mouth shut, and then you'd see his nostrils flare tremendously and hold

125

there, sucking in and then expelling a great draft of air. It must have been like sneezing through your ears or something.

I yawn again, chinking my body into the swing snugly, and as I yawn the din of the world shuts down. I can't hear a thing. Does this happen to everybody? I finish yawning and the earth comes back on, somebody turns up the volume.

I close my eyes. There is the dusk of my eyelashes and then the full night. I hear the wind and feel it but know nothing else of what it does. Lord, I am sleepy.

Grandpa. He slept to let the rest of us know it. He raged when he retired. Air would shuffle in and out of his body like covey after covey of quail flushed. If sleep was originally for our own protection, protection from roving predators who couldn't detect us because we were still, how explain the common snore? Grandpa wouldn't have lasted past ten-thirty in the wild.

I used to watch him wake up. He'd fall asleep watching TV, and then wake up two or three times during the evening. It took him a full five minutes. It was like looking out a window waiting for somebody to drive up. His body would move, then his shoulders. Muscles would twitch in his cheek. Then his eyelids would gently open, roll back like winter before spring. And he would look straight ahead for a minute, then slowly around the room, like he'd never seen it, and finally at you, as if he'd finally arrived.

It's so nice sometimes just to be able to lie down and go to sleep. It's the great equalizer. But my mind couldn't care less. It's worn out. I turn a bit in my swing, and that's the last I recall.

And I wake up, touched, touching, weighted down. A deep sleep fell upon me and a woman is made. We are in the hearse, Mary and I, and she says, "Come on," but I hold her and say, "No, wait, just like this, let's not move, I'll stay here." And she slides back down, slowly, around and over me, on me. I bring my knees up behind her, so she can lean back against my thighs. She takes her hair in her hands and pulls it back, lets it fall forward again. She leans forward and kisses me on the nose.

We were in the parking lot of a theater in Louisville, and we had both decided, after the play, that we were too tired to drive back to Lexington. It was late. I'd parked under a street lamp, and so, after we'd climbed over the front seat into the back of the hearse and spread out the blankets, I drew the black curtains around the back windows. We undressed in the dark and lay next to each other between the covers. I held her hand. The street lamp shone faintly through the fogged windshield.

She said, "It's like camping out."

And I said, "I'm tired, but are we going to waste this opportunity?"

And she put her hair against my cheek and slid her hand slowly down my chest and into my shorts.

She kisses me on the nose, sitting on top of me, squirming. She can't sit still, and I giggle, and she says, "It's not funny, come on."

And I say, "No, I just want to stay like this from now on, us together."

My mind is a minnow tank.

The hearse has plenty of room in back, so she can sit up straight and still not touch her head to the ceiling. I run my finger along the seam of our hips, and reach down and entangle our hair. The street lamp shines on her pale chest.

"Can you see anything?" I ask her.

"No," she says, "just the red and green and yellow of a signal light up the street. Everything else is fog. You're breathing too heavily."

"*I'm* breathing too heavily?"

"Yeah."

And she puts her palms on my hip bones and pushes herself up, then drops slowly back down.

127

"Be still," I tell her. And run my hands up her sleek sides and under her breasts. "How do you know if you have cancer?" I say, and rub my finger around and around her nipple.

"What a question to ask."

"No, I heard it on the radio. You're supposed to check yourself for cancer. Have you done it?"

"Yes."

"How do you know?"

"You just feel around in a circle, like this, and feel for lumps. Here, you do it." And she picked up my hand and started it moving around her breast. I kneaded gently, around and around, and she said, "I should have known you like to play doctor."

And so when I reached her nipples, I took one in each hand and twisted them gently, back and forth, and said, "Calling Tokyo, calling Tokyo," till she squirmed out of my grasp.

"No lumps," I said.

And she said, "C'mon, Hart," and so we started again.

And the memory is over. Fled is that music. She was smooth running deep. In the bucket of my brain a life darts incessantly back and forth.

16

I WOKE UP, as always, unsure of where I was, past, present, future. A blast of light from the doorway chastened me, but I blinked back, and saw there, made out, the silhouette of my grandfather, eclipsing the fluorescent light from the kitchen.

What? I opened my mouth but nothing came out. "Hart?"

"What?" I said, and this time my throat worked.

He whispered back, "Hart, get up, son, we've got a calf coming and I need you."

I rubbed my eyes with my fists and rolled out of bed, sat up. The sheets were clammy with the hot August night and I threw them back, away from my legs.

"Get dressed. I'll be here in the kitchen. Bring you a blanket." And he closed the door halfway and went into the kitchen.

I looked over at the clock. Three-thirty in the morning. I put on some jeans and a T-shirt, my sneakers. Everything was blunted, soggy. It was so hot. I held my arms out so they wouldn't touch my sides. My hair felt like a wet dog.

Grandpa was waiting for me in the kitchen, anxious, standing at the sink sipping a cup of coffee. I nearly had to close my eyes for the light.

"Where's your blanket?" he said.

I opened my eyes a little more. "What do I need a blanket for?"

"It's rained a little out and the ground's wet. I think we're in for a wait with her and we'll be sitting awhile. I might need to send you after the vet."

I turned, still blinking, and went after my blanket. It had rained. No wonder the humidity. I wadded my blanket up in my arms and went back to the kitchen. The whole idea was still a little foggy.

"What now?" I asked. "What's going on?"

"Here," he said, "drink this." And he handed me a cup of coffee.

"I don't like coffee."

"Drink it anyway. It's hot and'll hurt your tongue, wake you up."

I took one sip and set it back down.

"Well, c'mon, then," he said, and I followed him out

129

the door. We made Zeke stay in the house. I thought about Ford and Moto, but Grandpa said to let them sleep. The whole world felt like a damp corner. I pulled my pants up, jumping up in the air a little bit to get the cuffs out from under my heels. Grandpa was already off, leaning forward, hands shoved in pockets, his hat brim tipped low over his brow. He moved like he was on a New York sidewalk, in a fog, trudging along like some lost detective, walking out the mystery. The moon made his shadow. I was a little better after a minute. The walking made a wind that would have been hard-pressed to lift a dust mote but it was still something. We walked down the dirt road along the tobacco and up into a hillside field where the cattle were. I had the blanket and Grandpa carried a lantern in one hand at his side. I could hear the kerosene swish in it as it swung. When we got into the field he stopped and had me hold the lantern while he fished for a match, struck it and lit the wick. He pushed the glass back down over the flame and the lantern hummed. The sky was clear, bright and clear, stars and nearly a full moon, and big white moths around the light. They kept up with us as best they could. The fescue snapped back, flinging water as we swept through it. It soaked us from the waist down. When a drop splashed against the lamp it would fizzle, and slide down the glass boiling.

The cow was in the tall grass, on her side. She'd smoothed down a wide circle, rolling around.

"How'd you know she was here?" I asked him. He was holding the lamp high in the air, squinting. We stood a good fifteen or twenty feet from her.

"I just happened on to her," he said.

"At three in the morning?"

"I always check on 'em." He walked all around the trodden circle, holding the lamp up, and finally made it back around to me and my blanket.

"She acts like she's hurting," he said, and ran his hand over his face, the stubble of his chin and cheek. "We just

130

have to wait. I didn't find any blood or anything, but she acts funny. She's awful little."

He sat the lantern down and we spread the blanket out on the ground. "I'd let you go on back, but if she has trouble you might have to run down and call Doc."

I lay down. He sat up at the edge of the blanket and reached over and turned down the lantern. It gave off just enough light to make out the cow, and draw in every bug for forty miles. I was willing to go right back to sleep, but Grandpa was nervous or something, anxious. He wanted, of all things, to talk. Maybe it was the dark, that we couldn't really see each other. He knew I was on my back.

"I just wish I knew more," he said. He was talking about cows. "That Doc knows everything. If we need him we'll get him. He won't mind." He kept rubbing his chin.

I said, "Don't worry about it. You want me to go call him now?"

"No, no, we'll wait awhile. She may be fine. Some of them just take a little time. We'll wait here."

Moths circled the lantern in white fluttering arcs. A smaller green bug, metallic, buzzed through the light and was gone in a few seconds, then buzzed back around the other side. A comet. I lay back, my hands locked behind my head, waiting for something to crawl across my neck, or dive in my ear. Grandpa swatted at something that tried to get up his nose and I laughed, just snorted quickly, once, and he whacked the sole of my shoe.

"Hey!"

"Hey," he said. "I remember you," he said. "You came out of the maternity sound asleep. It wasn't nothing to you then either. This is something."

"I know it's something. We've watched fifty of 'em already this summer."

"Well, they're all something. You don't know what something is."

"I do too."

131

He sighed. "No, you don't."

"Do too."

"I went down there on the airplane to be there when you came."

"I appreciate it. What?"

"I mean I got on the airplane for the first time in my life and was there, in the room outside, when your mother ran you outside. And they said you were asleep even then. They had to wake you up to show you it'd happened, and then by the time your father got you out to me you were asleep again."

"I just had my eyes closed. I was remembering it already. There was this bright flash of light but it was cold."

"You was a little pink puffed-up hunk of bologna."

"Do we have to talk about this now?"

"As fat as you was, you come awful easy. Your momma has my hips. She didn't get your grandma's hips. Your grandma had a lousy set of hips, too thin for babies. She had an awful long time with your mom. We were up with her for a day and a night trying to get her born. She wouldn't have any part of it. It was something."

"So that's why you only had Mom, the one kid—Grandma's hips?"

"No. We tried other times, just like your momma and daddy. You try until you can't stand the sadness of it anymore."

He got up and moved the lantern out farther from us. The bugs swarmed around him. They followed him back to the blanket but wandered, one by one, back to the lamp.

I said, "Momma kept miscarrying."

He nodded. And as if he'd forgotten the cow, why we were out here in the hot night, he suddenly jumped up and went to look at her. He knelt at her side and felt her abdomen.

"I wish she'd do something. She won't get up and she won't contract."

132

He rubbed the cow's flank and then walked slowly, bent over, back to our blanket and sat down. I lay on my back and listened to him breathe. A moth wandered over me and behind Grandpa toward the lantern, bridging stars. Every beat of his wings was an adventure. A sparse cloud blundered under the moon and the moon shone through it. It was like a worn place in the night.

"I mean to say you never know what's going to happen," he said. "And there's not a lot we can do about it, you and I. It's all left to them. Your grandma," he said, "talked about dinner all through her time. Jabbered. What she needed to fix and what I wanted. Always worrying about feeding somebody. That table in the kitchen, she threw out our oak table and brought that one in, claiming it the marvel of the century because it didn't need a tablecloth, wouldn't ring. You know that?"

I shook my head.

"Yeah," he said, "marvelous woman, your grandma. Pretty, and"—and he turned around to me in the dark—"and soft a thing as . . ." He turned back slowly. "I don't know what. I don't know what would've happened to me if I hadn't married her."

"How'd you meet her?" I said it as unobtrusively as possible, slipping it in between his breaths and holding mine.

"She worked in a drugstore and I asked her to go to a show that evening after work. She said fine, to meet her there at closing. And I came in just as she was sneaking out the back door. Caught her red-handed. Had her coat draped over one arm going out the back way."

"She didn't want to go?"

"I caught her though, you see. I was quicker than her." He looked over at the cow. "I think I'm going to send you to call."

"You want me to go now?"

"No. Let's wait a bit more. I just wish she'd do something. I hate to wake Doc up in the middle of the night."

He rubbed his jaw again and picked at his nose. "Now that girl of yours"—and he was speaking louder—"what do you hold on to when you kiss her? She's too skinny."

"I can't believe you said that. You're a grandpa, you don't say things like that."

"Well, I say anything I please." And he rubbed at his eyes. He got up and went to the cow again and called back at me. I got up and went to him. "Go on and call. Tell him I'm awful sorry for getting him up. She's not doing anything and she smells bad."

"You just now noticing that?"

"No, she smells wrong bad. Tell him where we're at. He knows the farm."

I started off toward the house, moving the hay out of the way carefully with my hands. Then he said, "Go on, Hart," which meant run, and so I did.

I ran down through the field, trying to remember the holes and ditches, the fescue splashing water against my face and shirt, and finally hit the dirt road where I could let it out and I ran. The screen door slapped behind me and woke up Zeke under the kitchen table and I had to push him away to get at the phone, dialing it with my wet fingers.

The vet said, "Tell Gude next time he buys a herd like this I'm gonna shoot him." I smiled and put the phone down and started back up the hill. I left Zeke barking at the screen door. Winded, and the grade against me, I looked down at the ground. I would glance up occasionally to get my bearings on the lantern and then hang my head down again. I stumbled and slid up the hill like a bound moth. Grandpa was still there by the cow.

"Anything?" I said.

"She won't do anything. Doc coming?"

"Be here in a few minutes."

He stood up and wandered around the open space in the grass. "Can't do anything but wait. The sun'll be up in a little. See better then."

134

I went back over to the blanket and collapsed. I was lathered and disgusted with the wet heat. I lay on my back and breathed up at the sky.

The vet came soon. Grandpa had only said, "Well, I wonder where he is?" twice, before we saw the headlights of his truck bounce into the driveway and come toward us through the grass. He left the headlights on and pointed the truck at the cow. When he got out he said, "Gude," and Grandpa almost dragged him by the arm over to the cow.

"She ain't right," he said. Grandpa and I stood over the vet as he looked at her. Then he went back to his truck for a pair of gloves, long thin latex gloves that folded up past his elbow. He had us hold the cow. I put my knee on her neck and Grandpa rested on her back legs. She mooed and barked but didn't move much. She was too weak. The vet ran his hand and arm up slowly into her, feeling for the calf. Grandpa held tightly on, and kept looking at the vet.

"Well?"

And the vet said, "This is bad, Gude."

"The calf turned around wrong? Why don't she contract?"

"She already has." And the vet started to draw his arm out of her. The cow struggled and I pressed my knee down on her neck, while her big eyes swung wildly up at me. He said, "I've got a front hoof," and he pulled his arm and hand back and the hoof and front leg of the calf started to draw out, matted with blood and afterbirth. It drew out about ten inches and then ripped loose, fell to the ground. Grandpa grunted. "She tried to have this calf two or three days ago. He's dead and rotted." The smell was awful. I covered my nose while the vet reached up in her again, and drew out a handful of flesh. "We have to get all of it out. It'll just come a handful at a time. It rots real quick inside." Most of the calf was unrecognizable. Grandpa just sat there watching.

135

I said, "It was just like she was going into labor." I was scared for Grandpa.

The vet said, "There was no way for you to know except the smell. She's heavily infected and we'll need to give her several shots, but she should make it."

Grandpa still didn't say anything. He just watched the vet work, draw hand after hand of bone and flesh out of her and throw it in a pile away from us.

"Now, Gude, don't let your dog get into this stuff."

"No, I won't. I'll bury it," he said. And he raked his sleeve across his face. And then he said, "Aw, Jesus. Poor, poor cow. Poor cow." And he rubbed the heifer along the flank. He was all bleary-eyed, like a drunk.

The vet said, "Well, now, Gude." And then all he could do was go on with his work.

And the beam of headlights flush on our faces, casting our bowed shadows long and darkly against the deep grass beyond, and between us the shadow of heat rising. Then behind the truck the dawn coming. Wait a minute. Wait a minute. Wait. I held my breath and pressed my knee into the heifer's neck, hard, and thought about him raising my mother, and about him raising my mother, for the most part, alone.

17

AND ALTHOUGH I am anchored down by my thinking to a tedious diameter on the surface, my body is untethered, gullish, bound to no single medium. Man is the only great primate that can swim. I am always leaving a wake.

After our naps I put the mail in its pigeonhole and head for the old truck. It's still daylight, but the bluff of summer has gone out of the air and I can almost look the sun in the face for the coward that it is. It's at eye level already. The truck is a 1954 Chevrolet, still pulling but needs her hull scraped. The road salt of twenty-eight winters has broken her back and she sags amidframe and won't haul much more than me and Zeke without taking water when we go over a bridge. I yank on the door, and then give it another yank, and it opens. I stand out of the way. Zeke, always ready when he smells a trip, does a smooth leap and glissade onto the bench seat, sits with his front paws balanced and braced on the edge of the leather and looks out the windshield. He is ready, faithful seadog. I would mount him on my hood if he would have it, let his big soft ears flap in the wind, his stiff lip and crinkled brow guide and protect me. But as it is, he'd rather just go along for the ride. I am the pilot, and the road itself is our navigator, the asphalt wake of the last truck to pass. I run my hand through my hair for appearance's sake.

I put my foot on the starter and she sputters up, rocking and puffing, so I reach out and close the door. Zeke is still eyes forward. He never had a doubt. I sigh, impoverished, pop the clutch. And we are on the road, moving toward Decatur, making our own wind. Who'd have thought it possible? If I'd known it was this easy, I'd have gone hours ago. It always surprises me, the opportunity and ability to go. Zeke leans his big shoulder on the door and puts his head out the window, stretches his neck and snout far out into the wind. Nature made him a streamlined model, intent. Where was the foresight? Who'd have known even a paltry two hundred years ago that a dog's head would someday need to be able to knife through a constant fifty-mile-an-hour truck wind? He leans out the window and thrills in the effortless speed, mouth shut, ears pinked back, eyes slotted. I try it, holding on to the top of the big steering wheel with one hand and poking my head out the window. But it's no use. My face was never meant for more than a good steady ten-mile-per-hour trot; it slices through the wind like a lawn chair; my eyes water and my ears refuse to fold back. So I bring my face back inside out of the weather.

The truck bounces forward on its way and I still steer with one hand. There is about six inches of play in the wheel, and so even on a straight stretch I steer for my life, and a sharp curve has to be thought about a couple of minutes ahead of time. But one hand can handle all of this, a good deal of it. With my free hand I pull the stuffing out of the old seat between me and Zeke. A tiny pinch at a time, simply because it's somehow irresistible, that I roll into a tight little ball and flip out the window. A trail for someone to follow.

We pass five miles of farms and finally spill into Decatur over the bridge that spans the Muskatatuck. Zeke and I hold up our feet. We wash down through town past the college and the courthouse and a hard right another two blocks to the Co-op. There are four or five pickups already out front and I pull in among them, a convoy of farm transports. Zeke and I fall out, and before he gets any ideas I pat the bed of the truck and he, grudgingly, jumps in.

"Now you stay," I say and walk toward the door. The thing to do is not look back. I don't, and he lets out a high-pitched whine as I go in, to let me know I'm the heartbreaker I am.

Inside it is cool. I walk down the nut-and-bolt aisle and find myself wishing I had one of each. Then up the cattle aisle, where I pick up a box of worming pills and a gun for them, and give a grimace for the emasculator tools with their tiny rubber bands. The tool stretches a little rubber band (the kind kids put on their braces) so it will get over a set of testicles, and then lets it go. I walk bowlegged through the rest of the store, and up to the sales counter. John Thomas is there, in his "Co-op—You Own It" cap.

"Hello, Hart, this all?"

"No. I've got Grandpa's old tobacco setter up in the barn, but the hose on it, the hose that goes from the fertilizer tank to the plants as you set them, is rotted and I need a new one. Have you got those?"

"Sure," he says, and disappears through the double doors behind him. And before I can turn around to get a good look at whoever else is in the store, he is back, coiling up a piece of red rubber hose.

"There you go." He is always smiling. "Anything else?"

"Yeah. I'll need a couple of salt blocks and another fifty pounds of dog food," I said.

"That dog of yours eats up all the profit." And he writes up a ticket and I pay for the stuff I already own. "Just pull up to the dock and I'll get this other for you." I put the ticket in my shirt pocket and head toward the door through the galvanized tub aisle. Boy. They are new and shiny and I want one of each.

I hold open the door for an old woman, and as she thanks me Zeke nearly knocks me over from behind.

"What are you doing out of the truck?" I yell at him. He is always getting out of the truck.

Then someone says, "Don't yell at him. I let him out," and I look up. It is John Thomas' daughter, Penny. She helps out at the Co-op. Zeke runs, tail wagging, back to her, and she kneels down and rubs his face. "Good ol' Zeke. Mean ol' Hart. You're like a drink of water, aren't ya, boy?" And she scratches his ears.

I push myself into a frown. Pen is one of these girls who's always got her hands shoved in her back pockets. She's always smiling and walking up to you and slamming her hip into yours and saying, "When are we going to Reno?" or, "When are we going to Texas?"

I get in the truck and pull around to the dock and her dad hands me the dog food and salt blocks. I set them in back and call for Zeke, and he comes running, scoots up onto the seat. Pen walks over and reaches in through the window and rubs his nose.

"Good boy," she says, and Zeke pivots his head toward me, and if a dog can grin and look like Humphrey Bogart, he does. I start the truck, and Penny backs up.

"See ya, Hart," she says, and I wave at her.

What I mean to say, as we pull out of the gravel lot and begin our bashful return, is I mean I think she uses too much makeup around her eyes. She's got these pretty blue eyes and puts makeup all around them. I step on the gas, and turn left at the courthouse, and wonder, why does she do that?

18

"MEET George Jetson, dadatadadatadadatada," I said.

And Moto said, "Jane, his wife."

And Ford, "His boy, Elroy."

"Daughter, Judy." That was me.

And Moto again, "Rot rabrout mree, Rastro?"

And Ford, "I bet Zeke could whip hell out of Astro."

"Rastro."

"Rastro. Right. Rorry."

"Rokay."

We drove northeast out of Texas that September, our left arms baked, through the flats of Arkansas and across the Mississippi, up Route 51 through Tennessee, over Kentucky Lake and then toll road all the way to school. We were always fishing for quarters, and in between toll booths we'd lose our minds on cartoons and Big Red. "Some circumstantial evidence is very strong, as when you find a trout in the Big Red," I said at a gas station to Moto, after he came out of the restroom and took a Big Red from Ford. Ford had cornered a minnow in a bait tank and slipped it down through the pop-top hole in the can. Moto smiled and took a good drink. I couldn't take anymore. Ford was a little green himself. I grabbed the can and poured it out on the asphalt. The minnow got stuck sideways for a while but finally came out too. He flopped around till I got hold of him and pitched him back in the tank.

Then I looked at Moto. His lips were all screwed up. Then he said, "It's okay. I accidentally, one night this summer, peed on one of y'all's toothbrush. I got away from myself. Don't let this minnow thing bother you. I feel better now. The world is, once again, in balance."

And so we went on, stabilized, poised, all three of us rubbing our mouths. I drove the rest of the way into Lexington, with the chauffeur's cap on. Ford would lean his torso out the flower windows, arms draped down the fenders, and play dead. Moto let one naked foot peek from the back doors. It was my job to look like I was on just another overbooked delivery. I drove on, snapping a cassette in and cranking the volume: Otis Redding's "Sittin' on the Dock of the Bay," that we'd recorded ten times on the same tape. It played over and over. And we sang when we didn't play dead. We died with infectious grins, and people in their passing slowed in their passing, grinning. If their windows were down I'd look over solemnly and scream, "Wear your seat belt, for God's sake!"

We gave ourselves up for dead and so the miles slipped by, till Lexington fell within our lugubrious shadow. We pulled into the Fraternity House parking lot and, at last, the long summer was over. I got out and kissed the ground of campus. I carried my bags upstairs, shook Rank's extended hand, screamed at Wyeth when he came up behind and grabbed me by the hair of my armpit, and then I went to bed. I wanted to sleep through the next twelve hours. Mary's flight was due in the morning. I rolled into the newly spread sheets and the last thing I heard was Ford telling Rank to "get the hell away from my face."

I woke up the next morning ache-ridden and foul-mouthed. It sounded like somebody was using my ear for a cereal bowl. It was Ford, at his mirror, taking the cellophane off a new toothbrush.

"You get me one?" I asked.

"On your dresser."

"Money's in my pants."

"Already got it."

"You gonna knife Rank this semester?"

"I wouldn't have come back if I'd remembered him. I thought he was gonna move to another room."

"Who'd take him?"

"I bet he's gonna try out all the stuff he learned this summer on us."

"If you feel like you might knife him, let me know."

He shrugged, and I left him there at his mirror to go take a shower. I was in and out in less than two minutes, dressed and at the airport in another twenty. I only had an hour to wait for Mary. I was really beginning to take her for granted.

She came off that ship like the curl of a wave, spume and spindrift, white, cool with the sun through her blue, folding in on me. I turned around, and saw it was too late, too far back to the beach to run. So I stood there and spread my arms and she drenched me, sundress and body, freckles, and although I held my ground I was again gone under, and for breathing I vibrated. I'd met her at the door and as she slammed into me I picked her up and pressed her back to the wall, behind the door, and she wrapped her legs around my thighs and we held.

When I let her talk she said. "It's just like the movies, but better."

142

"Tons better," I said, and she let her legs drop down to the ground and I backed up a step so she could smooth the front of her sundress.

She said, "Luggage."

And I took her hand. "Nice dress," I said. "When can we take it off?"

"You bring the hearse?"

"Yeah," I said. "I'll run out and get the air conditioner going."

And she laughed. "Not for that. I've got all kinds of luggage. Lord, Hart."

"I sure missed you, girl. Christ, I love sundresses."

"The luggage, Hart."

"The luggage, Hart. Right. Do you want to go get your stuff at Grandpa's from here or drop this stuff off first?"

"Let's take this back to the dorm. Then I can change before we go down."

"Good idea," I grinned.

"Oh, Hart." I couldn't believe it. She was shy again. She wrapped her legs around me at the gate and now she remembered we hadn't seen each other in three months and she was shy again. We picked up her luggage and started toward the hearse. I was trying to carry three bags, listen to her tell me about some piece of music she'd worked on all summer, never take my eyes off her gorgeous face, and walk at the same time. A little kid must've walked right under me. I felt him with my knee and lifted that whole leg wide into the air so I wouldn't crush him, and fell myself, in a long swooping knock over two chairs and an ashtray almost save myself but no there I go with the loss of a sturdy handhold, fall. I fell for about twenty feet. People were diving out of the way. I lifted my head up from the tile looking for the kid. He was on the floor too. I jumped up and ran back to him and bent down. He was such a little kid. His mother was ten feet away and coming hard.

I said, "Are you okay, little kid?" I was scared to death he had a concussion or something. He rubbed his head, then his arm, and looked okay, but then his mom got there, with her high-pitched voice, and he started bawling.

I said, "I think he's okay. I'm awful sorry."

I expected to get the full treatment, told how careless I was and then an "Oh, don't worry about it," with a prim, sarcastic twist of mouth, but it didn't come. She apologized to me, said, "We step on him three or four times a day ourselves. He thinks it's a sport. Diving under your feet." Then she smiled and went on, dragging the kid. I felt like saying, "You're such a nice lady." Instead I went back to Mary and the bags.

"I thought I'd killed him," I told her.

"Luckily," she said, "you only knocked the airport out of service for a day or two."

I set the chairs I'd turned over back up and by that time a guy was sweeping up the gravel from the ashtray. I picked up the bags again and said to him, "Sorry."

"All right," he said.

And we went on to the University. She'd gotten a room on the third floor of the Tower this semester, coming down in the world. We crowded onto the elevator with about ten other girls and their luggage and went up. It took about two seconds to get to her floor. No time to calm at all, I thought. Her room was just like the old one, just 120 feet lower. You couldn't see the lights of the city.

"You'll be able to save yourself in case of fire," I said. "If you can't"—and I put down her luggage on the bed as she opened drawers and closets—"If you can't get down the stairs, you can break the window with your chair and jump." I was looking out the window. I was sort of talking senselessly.

"With my lousy ankles?" she said, and she closed the door on the hallway. I turned around and she was standing in the middle of the room, stepping out of her sandals, with her arms sticking straight up in the air. The sundress was a pullover.

144

"Okay," she said, smiling.

"I won't be able to last a minute."

"It's okay." And she jangled her arms and hands above her. "Come on, I just want to see your tan lines."

And we took the bags off the unmade bed, and made love there, and it was grand. She followed my tan lines, kissing there, and I did the same for her, and we were there forever, it seemed, skin to skin, rolling back the long summer, till her stomach began to grumble. I laughed, and she said, "I couldn't eat what they gave me on the plane. I'm starving."

"Pancake & Egg?" I asked.

"Never again," she said. "Let's find a supermarket." She'd decided not to go back to work. The extra scholarship would be enough.

"We need to go by the Fraternity House. Moto and Ford said to bring you by."

"What do they want?"

"Just to say hi."

She started to put on her underwear and I said, "Let me," and so I dressed her, snapped her bra, yanked up her jeans, and buttoned her blouse. Then I put in her earrings, which gave me the willies, and combed her glorious hair.

"Thanks," she said. I was still as naked as the last left-over clap in a theater. So she dressed me. It was a weird feeling. I hadn't had anyone zip up my pants since I was eight.

We had started to leave when Mary looked back into the room. There were boxes and bags spread out all over, nothing put up. She said, "I never get anything done when you're around."

"Sorry."

"I'll bet."

We plummeted three floors and walked to the Fraternity House. I tried to act cool but lost it, was too far gone with happiness at her side. I improvised along the sidewalk, ran at trees and walked up as far as I could, sneaked up behind her and clutched her ribs.

"Let's forget school," I said. "Let's forget Moto and Ford and your stuff at Grandpa's and just go." I talked and danced my way all the way to the front yard of the house. Moto and Ford were outside pitching the Nerf.

Moto saw Mary first, threw his hands up in the air and said, "Mary!" and gave her a hug. "I've missed you so!" He was being an asshole, pretending he was me. After he was through, Ford threw his hands up in the air too and said, "Mary!" and laid her over the hood of a car.

"All right," I said.

"Hi," Mary said; then, "We're going down to see Gude. You guys want to go?"

"You talking about Scatter?" Ford said.

"Yes."

"Without the least bit of hesitation," Moto said, "I think I can refer you to hell. I fixed everything on that place twice this summer. It'd all just break if I went down there again. And I believe I represent my fellow slave, Ford, here, as I speak."

"Yeah," Ford said. "Besides, we've got to think up something to do to Rank this evening."

"Besides," Moto went on, "we've got to pitch the Nerf this afternoon, Hart. Anyone can see that."

I bipped my forehead with the heel of my palm.

"C'mon, Hart," Mary said, "I'm starving." I bipped my forehead with the heel of my palm.

And she was swinging the door open before I'd even stopped at the supermarket.

"What do you want?" I asked, as she tore down the aisles.

"A cheese sandwich."

I stopped. Yuck. "I'll meet you at the register," I said, and went to find myself something edible. A little jar of green olives, some saltines, a bag of Doritos and some bean dip, and a Big Red. I moved up behind her in the fruit aisle and watched her pluck a grape from the bin and pop it in her mouth.

"Mary!"

"What!" She swung around, one cheek swollen with the grape.

"You're a grape-stealer!"

"I was hungry!"

"I'd never have picked you for a grape-thief."

"You're so witty."

"I'll bet if you find an open bag in the candy aisle, you take a couple malted-milk balls too."

"Yes. I do. Stop." And she held her forearm over her eyes. There was a loaf of French bread in her raised hand, and a package of cheese in the other.

"Well," I said, sighing, "I'm gonna have to report this to the store manager. I'm glad I've finally found out what side of the track your morals are on." And I turned and walked toward the registers.

She scooted up behind me. "You won't tell, will you? I'll make mad, passionate love to you among the fresh vegetables if you won't."

"Deal," I said, and stuck my hand in her back pocket. "A trick for the price of a grape." I knew I probably shouldn't have said it as soon as I did.

"Hart, that isn't funny." And she pulled away, and up to the counter.

When we got out to the hearse I put the key in the ignition and said, "I'm sorry. A dumb thing."

"A dumb thing."

I felt so intolerably stupid and persecuted. The way a kid would feel. But as we drove on, she ate her cheese sandwich and helped me with my stuff, and when we were through she cleared everything off the seat and put her head in my lap.

I said, "I never, ever think of you that way."

"I know. I shouldn't have been mad. I'm just tired. Tell me when we get to Gude's."

147

"Okay." I drove on with her head in my lap, and thought that too, that she shouldn't have been mad.

Grandpa met us outside as he always did. The house wasn't his theater. He, like all the old chieftains, liked to meet in the open.

We got out of the hearse and the first thing he said, holding his hat on his head, was, "It's gonna rain for sure," and then he pointed toward the north. We looked and saw nothing, blue skies and a few cirrus clouds way up high. "Mary!" And she gave him a hug. "Y'all hungry?" I groaned and Mary told him no. "Well, honey, I've got your box out of the closet and it's all ready to go."

"Thanks, Gude. I'd have hated to carry all that junk home and back. Hart's going to show me all the new cows."

"Calves, honey."

"Calves," she said.

"We've had another since you went home, Hart. I think he was the last one. Most of the little ones are in the second pasture. But y'all better hurry. It's gonna rain." And he grabbed his hat again and pointed to the north, as if the gestures had to go with the words to give them any meaning at all.

We started up behind the house and through the tobacco, which would need cutting soon, and on up into the first pasture. The wind was blowing and it was a little cold for September. I took Mary's hand and led her up through the grass, fragrant and full of bugs. Swallows swooped around us, hoping we'd kick an insect or two up to them.

"I have some music I want to play for you," she said, and she took her hand from mine to talk about it. "I spent all summer on it. I was down in the living room with the piano, just fooling around, and it started all by itself. My folks even like it." She was smiling and watching her feet walk.

"Yeah?" I said.

"Yeah."

148

I slipped through the barbed-wire fence and held two strands wide for her. The cows were down the hill a bit. "Look at 'em," I said. "Ain't they wonderful?" Almost every cow had a little spindly copy of itself at its side. We moved down among them and I pounced on a calf that was slow getting up. The heifer stood, square-shouldered, about ten feet away and bawled. Mary came to us timidly, and I said, "Don't you just love him? Ain't he little?" I sat on one knee with one arm under the calf's neck and the other over his back. He stuck his little pink nose up in the air and bawled. Mary reached down and felt his ear like it was a piece of cloth.

"He's awful cute," she said. "How's he walk on those puny legs?"

"Like this," and I stood up, letting him go, and he stumbled to his mother and she turned to lead him away.

I looked at Mary and suddenly felt like a hug, so I walked over and did that. "C'mon," I said, "let's get your stuff and go home. We can slip over to the conservatory and hear your music. I love your music."

"You love everything."

"No, I don't."

"You do too. You'd kiss a snake if you thought he was sad."

"I would not."

"You would too. You even loved that little kid who tripped you in the airport."

We started back up the hill and I put my arm over her shoulder. I said, "Hum what you did this summer."

"You can't hum piano music."

"Well," I said, "do it in pinks and punks and ponks." And she smiled, and leaned over and kissed me on the ear, and then hummed a little.

"See," I said, "I love that."

"Oh, Hart, you love everything."

"So?" I was in a grand mood.

She put her arm around my back and pressed into me.

149

19

WE COME HOME, Zeke and I, famished warriors, to the hurrahs of chickens. They cluck and strut at our unexpected return. I park the truck and roll up Zeke's window after he jumps out. He always forgets, and you never can tell when it might rain. I pick up his dog food and carry it to the porch, which he takes a great interest in, and then back to the truck for the salt blocks and pills. They go on the side porch too. We'll take them to the cattle in the morning. I won't use the tobacco setter this spring. I've sold the poundage to a family down the road, and they'll raise it. But there's no use in letting the equipment go, and that's why I bought the new hose. I carry it into the garage and set it on the bench. That's for tomorrow too.

When we come back out of the garage, Asia whinnies. I'd forgotten all about her. She is leaning up against the gate, her ears perked at us. And so we go and stow her away too, with another bucket of grain. She backs away as I open the gate, but follows me up to her stall and walks in without any trouble at all. I say, "Well, aren't you a pleasure to work with," and pat her smooth, warm neck. Then I close her door, and drag the two big barn doors across the tracks to a close. Zeke runs out the little door then, afraid that I'll shut him up with those rats for the night. I close that door too when he is clear, turn the little two-by-four latch, a block on a nail, so even the almighty wind can't open it. And as we walk back across the barnyard we lose our shadows in the dusk. They simply walk out from under us and disappear.

Up on the porch Zeke tries to squeeze in the door with me. He knows I'm going to fix myself something to eat. He jams his head between my hip and the door frame and pushes. "No, Zeke, no." And I finally spurt beyond him and put my hand in front of his face while I shut the door.

The dog has the mind of a sneak. He ought to be a carrier for stolen diamonds, or secret war plans. If he can do Bogart, he can do Peter Lorre too. "Pleez, Mr. Hart, pleez, just let me hide in the house. I won't be the least bother to you, pleez. Say you'll let me, Mr. Hart. Pleez."

Dinner is never a problem. I always limit myself to only two items. Any more than that, and I end up eating them all separately anyway. I am not a coordinated cooker. Heating times and temperatures seem extremely confusing, and so I usually end up cranking up the oven to about 475 degrees and opening the door every minute or two to check. It seems to work, although I haven't had any eyebrows for about a year now. Tonight I fry up some okra and cut open a cantaloupe. And since it is a little cold, a cup of hot chocolate. I like to eat with my plate in my lap, so I try to get around stuff where you have to use a knife. I am thinking about sharpening the sides of my spoons on the grinder in the garage: an all-purpose eating tool that leaves one hand free for a magazine.

I eat, swab my face with a paper towel, and wash my few dishes. Eating is a little-enough price to pay for living, but the dishes are a heavy tax. I throw them overboard every night, but my sink is too shallow. Zeke stands up on his hind legs and peers in the window over the sink as I wash. He breathes on the murky panes and fogs them up. "Get down from there," I say, and wring out my washrag.

Then I remember the other dirty rags and take a tour through the house turning on lights, looking for socks. I have never been able to understand why the consistent proximity of my two feet to each other bears no relationship to the proximity a pair of socks has that I wore the day before. I will find one in the living room under the couch and the other behind the toilet in the bathroom. My brain must have some mechanism that forces me into movement when I remove a sock. But I find them all at last and toss everything—towels, socks, jeans—into the washer. And decide while I'm at it, since the washer is in the bathroom, to wash myself too.

I am a mess. I run my hand through my hair and things fall out of it. My pockets are full of seed. If I were to take a shower with my clothes on, I'd probably sprout. But I don't chance it, strip and throw the clothes in the washer too. I start to take my watch off but then remember it is safe at 200 feet and leave it on. And I shower, a stock-still swimming, a localized rain. And come out a new man, born and throwing myself a towel at the same time. I dry off, look in the mirror for any new scars, warts, wrinkles, or pimples, and pronounce myself still blasphemously young. The day didn't take my youth. Perhaps prolonged it. I think I'll be able to start again tomorrow. I finish up, and walk down the hall to my room and dress again, and the phone rings. I run down the hall to Grandpa's study.

"Hello?"

"Hi, honey."

"Hi, Mom."

"How are you?"

"Fine. I got the books from Dad. Did you know he sent me his copy of Crane?"

"Yes. He told me. He thought you'd get more use out of it than he did."

"Well, I'm gonna call Pap in a day or two and tell him I like it. I think he'd like that."

"I'm sure. How're the cows? You hate 'em yet?"

"No, not yet. They're not ripping down fences yet. Ask me again this summer. I went into town and got a couple of salt blocks for 'em this afternoon. I think they're all healthy."

152

"How's Zeke?" She asks all the questions I would ask.

"Oh, he's fine. He's getting to think he's a house dog, though. I've been letting him inside too much."

"Hart, don't let him tear up any of Dad's furniture."

"He doesn't. I watch him."

"Your dad and I have been talking. We're thinking about coming up for the whole summer, get away from the heat. What do you think?"

"Sounds great. Can he get off work that long?"

"Well, he's got almost two months of vacation and sick days saved up and they say he has to take them this year. They're not going to let people carry days over into the next year anymore."

"Yeah, Mom. You might as well take them."

"Well, we haven't looked at a calendar yet but I'll give you a call when we decide."

"Hey, have you seen Moto around?"

"No, I saw his folks a week or two ago. They said they're all fine."

"Well, if you see him tell him to give me a call."

"Okay. Anything else?"

"Where's Dad?"

"He's at Pap's."

"Tell him I'll need help this summer."

"Okay," she says, and then the phone beeps with another call. "That's somebody, Hart. I better go. Be good. I'll call you."

"Okay. Bye, Mom."

"Bye, bye, honey."

And I hang up the phone. She calls at a whim but I can always guess. I leave my hand on the receiver, thinking about them coming up, and look around Grandpa's study. The books on the shelves are mostly about farming of some kind: tobacco, cattle and grass, soil. A set of encyclopedias and a yearbook for every year since 1946. The yearbooks still come in his name and I still take them. It's an accumulation of knowledge I rarely refer to, a library for archaeologists that I dust. Up on top of his desk, on a little pedestal, is the helmet. The one from World War I, not his, but the German's. The guy that he killed. I used to think when I was a kid, that he kept it there sort of like a trophy, but then I realized that his medals, his uniform and helmet, he kept upstairs in a locked trunk. He never brought them out. He kept the helmet there on his desk to remind himself, I think. Every phone call he took, every letter he opened, every book he read was taken, opened, and read in the shadow of this man he'd killed. He used to tell us, while we worked, Moto and Ford and I, that we were lucky, that war was no longer "an advantageous pursuit."

I sit at his desk, and pick up his old field glasses from the war, and look out the dark window. It is evening now. The swallows are all perched on the electric line between the garage and the barn. There is something about the coming of night that makes animals queue. Humans in front of theaters, cows along a fence, birds on a ridge row. You watch his back and I'll watch yours. The night is a Serengeti and we are all on safari. Let us enter into the darkness in an orderly fashion. So we file past the open coffin.

I can imagine him, my age, younger, picking the glasses up, wrapping the strap around his wrist and leaning forward on his elbows, above the trench. I can see him bracing himself with his feet against the rear wall of the ditch, and trying not to breathe, holding the glasses up to his eyes and not breathing.

20

I DON'T REMEMBER the wind blowing, for instance. I
have to be careful here. But it seems the whole semester was breezeless, hot and slack in September
and cold and slack in November, never a cool time, no
autumn in between. I mean in the background of a memory there is always something, a sack scudding across the
street, a curl of hair faintly buffeted, but in this, in these,
stillness, just the memory itself, sweat and ice. Nothing
fell and nothing rose. We were all holding our breath for
a better time to breathe.

"You're such a sweet, sweet kid. Why do you even like
me?"

Even though there is no better time for breathing than
the present. I surfaced and sucked in, rolled over and
struck back across the pool. Swimming and not feeling
the water but the motion through it, the tug forward of
my own lungs. I was swimming for the speed of it, outfin-
ning eels and leeches and sharks, hard in for the shore,
hand over hand over the rope of the surface. I cracked
my knuckles against the cement wall and stood up in the
shallow end, holding on to the rim of the pool. My legs
were wobbly, even in the water, and my chest billowed
and fell limp, billowed. I held my palm to it for a moment
and then pulled myself up on the concrete. I looked
around for Mary but couldn't see her, and was worried
after a minute, thinking about the water, and got out. I
walked a few steps, and then saw her and so I stopped.

She was on the far side of the pool, her arms wrapped around her knees, watching me. I'd thought she was someone else. I was okay.

"You know, that day in The Pancake & Egg, I didn't expect liking you."

And I can't remember any inflection in her voice, just the way she parted her lips, slowly, and the sound issuing, or no sound at all, just the parting of her lips. And sometimes I would move in and press against her when there wasn't any sound and she would take me in. She bore my burden. Lover, lover, I would say.

"It was just so nice to have you."

Ford threw me a long arching Nerf pass that I had to lean over a bush to catch with one hand.

"See that?" I screamed back at him and Moto.

"It was the pass," Ford yelled.

I stopped in front of the science building and spun the Nerf up in the air in a smooth spiral and caught it behind my back. Ford and Moto finally caught up.

"We're gonna be late again," I said. Astronomy was the only class we all three shared that semester. Our different majors were beginning to split us up.

"God," Moto said, "I hate being late."

Ford said, "Well, let's just cut it. That guy drives me bored anyway."

"We already cut it twice," I said.

"If we keep cutting classes," Moto went on, "my ascension to genius level, which I am daily approaching, will be held up."

"Well, I don't think he likes to see us come in late with the Nerf in our hands," Ford said.

"Good point."

"Still we ought not to cut it," I said.

156

Ford bent down and picked up a wad of grass, sorted it out and then let most of it fall again. Then he put his fist up in our faces. Three blades of grass stuck up out of it. "Shortest blade doesn't get to cut and has to take and share notes in a good-humored fashion." I reached forward and drew a blade out, then Moto, and Ford held open his palm.

I tossed the Nerf to Moto and said, "Let's raid the Student Center."

And Ford said, "Wait, wait. I'll give one of you guys two bucks to take my place. What do you think?"

I held my palm out and said, "The money." He beamed and produced two wadded bills which I took, putting one in my pocket and the other in Moto's hand. "Come on," I said to Moto and we started inside.

Ford said, "What?" and "What?" and "Wait!" and followed us, glumly, into Astronomy. "Yawn," he said. "Bore me useless," he said, sneaking to the back of the room.

"I was doing so well and I wanted to share it."

"Where's Mary today?" Grandpa asked.

"She couldn't come down. She's working on a piece for a class. Practicing."

We were giving a few of the new calves shots. I ran them one at a time out of the barn lot into the barn and up into a chute. Grandpa slid the big needle into their flanks and pumped in the medicine, and then I let them back out of the chute. They ran, their hindquarters bouncing, out into the other side of the barnyard.

"These calves are gonna be trouble this winter, Hart. You wait and see. They've never been cold and aren't gonna be very big by then anyway. We'll have to watch them."

I nodded, and guided another calf into the chute. It was still hot, late in October, and I thought it would never

157

cool off. My clothes, arms, and face were matted with my sweat and calf hair. I kept running my forearm across my face.

"Why don't you sell them," I said. "Let somebody else winter them. You don't need the money." He didn't even bother to answer me. So I said, "I'll try to bring Mary when I come down next week."

He said, "Tell her I think she's the best idea since water running downhill."

And I didn't say anything for a while, nervous. I finally got it out, trying to sound as nonchalant as possible, saying it like I was talking about a cow or something, "You know, I think I love her."

And he said, acknowledging, nodding, affirming, "You do?"

"Yeah." And I punched a calf in the flank when he tried to back out of the chute, and drove him back up.

"I just need to practice some, okay, Hart? Please?"

And the sun and moon were overhead but I don't remember ever looking at them, only feeling them and seeing what they left on the ground, a feeble or glaring light. I remember the undersides of leaves, a tall building, the ceiling over my bunk. And a huge motion-picture screen. We'd come in late and found the theater full, only a few scattered single seats left in back, and so we sat in the empty front row and slumped down. We leaned back and looked up at the huge eyes and collars and during the show I reached over and held her hand. I remember it as a good picture.

"I know it seems sudden, like I haven't thought."

Ford got hold of a safari outfitters mail-order catalog somewhere, and he and Moto and I spent our last farthings on clothes and must accessories. It all came in one huge Apple Jack cereal box, and Ford carried it upstairs and into the room singing "The Lion Sleeps Tonight." We ravaged the box, tossing back cellophane, packing paper, and pins like so much earth scratched back. Everything was khaki and white: safari vests, shirts of Egyptian cotton, British army trousers, Gurkha shorts. They had Sri Lanka, Hong Kong, and Sierra Leone labels. Moto wore the Gurkha shorts (the Gurkhas were hired mercenaries for the British from Nepal—Ford liked the idea), a pith helmet, and a brass compass on a string around his neck. I put on my Gurkha hat, the kind that buttons up on one side, the kind they used in the "Rat Patrol," and my army trousers, and strapped a canteen over my shoulder. Ford wore the Dutch cap with its little round goggles that strapped above the brim and hung a brass telescope from his neck. I would have hated to have seen him behind a .50 caliber machine gun. We straightened our brims in the mirror, and Ford said, "Hup," and, "finally, a little adventure," and we strode out into the windless desert, the blasted earth, across campus, and into Astronomy class, sighing all the way, "a-wimoweh, a-wimoweh," to hand in our terrible report.

"Maybe it's that we're together so much."

Worse than the words her horrible silence. Say something.

"I just wish you didn't love me as much as you do."

And it seemed that time was just a field in which to narrow my vision, cord my stomach, slow my headlong gait. I contracted, waded through each day, and found my bunk, but did not explode. There didn't seem to be any need to talk and so I concentrated on listening, sure that I'd missed something in each sentence as the next was spoken. I just wanted to yell, "Wait, wait a minute."

*   *   *

"I hate myself for this."

I met old Ashpal, walking across campus; his glass eye bored a hole in me twenty feet away. And I thought that's what it's like, being that glass eye. We drew closer, his eye still recognizing me, and we passed, and I realized it was the wrong eye, that he never saw me, and I ran around behind him to the other side.

"Sir? How are you, sir?"

He stopped, and fixed on me, and said, "Ancient History, second period last semester: You're Hart."

"Yes, sir."

"How are you?"

"Just fine."

"Classes going well this term?"

"Fine."

"You hadn't decided on a major yet."

"I'm still not sure." I turned and walked with him. "Maybe History or English."

"The Arts. Nothing like the Arts to take refuge in." And he winked his one good eye at me, and I thought, what a chance he takes, winking, plunged into total darkness. "With History, English, you at least always know you're not alone."

"How are you, sir?"

"Fine, fine."

"I never did tell you how much I liked the class. I mean, I did."

"You were a good student, Hart. What about the other two wise men?"

"They're okay."

"Still star-searching?"

Jesus, I got nervous when professors started in with religion.

"We have an Astronomy class this semester."

"Give them my best."

160

"Yes, sir."

He started up the steps to his next class and never turned back to me but asked in a loud voice, "Do you recall anything?"

I yelled up at him, "I remember everything, sir."

"I could make love to you forever."

It wasn't only the wind but the rain too; where is that in my memory? The leaden gray of light but no water; where is that? The dew and mist, fog, morning rain, and afternoon thunder, the wipers on the hearse flicking back and forth; not with me. You know it must have rained. I must have held it in my palm and thrown off wet socks and pressed my face to the window when I woke. I must have cringed when I walked under the eaves, and jousted with my umbrella, seen a girl's stranded wet hair and her pale ears revealed, avoided a puddle, and arrived, winded, under cover.

"I wish I felt the other way. I wish I wanted to give in to it."

I was sitting on the carpet outside of the practice room, my elbows on my knees, reading. And I was okay for a while, reading and listening to the faint music from the sill, sitting outside the door. Her tutor showed up late, a guy the school had hired just for her. He was a fairly young guy, maybe thirty-five. He was supposed to be some kind of piano genius. He looked at me as he walked down the hall, and tapped the number on Mary's door still looking at me. He said, "Can I help you with something?"

And I said, "No, I'm just waiting on Mary."

"Well, we may be awhile." He had the door halfway open. Mary had stopped playing. I knew she could hear us.

161

"It's okay. I'll wait."

"It may be an hour or more."

"Fine."

"Well, you won't interrupt or disturb us, looking in the window?"

"No, I won't bother you. I'm just going to sit here." Who did this guy think he was? Why wasn't Mary saying anything? I knew she didn't like him, not at all. "Well, all right." And he shut the door. I looked back at my book, and then back up at the door, and I saw his hands at the window, and then a piece of sheet music. He'd taped the sheet music over the little square window. I stood up and threw the book the length of the hallway, walked across the hall and back to the door. I put my hand on the knob, even though I knew she didn't like him, that it was he who liked her. She'd called him a creep a dozen times. I put my hand on the knob, and then drew it away and backed across the hall again. I couldn't do anything. I shoved my hands in my pockets and stood there, and finally got fed up with my inability and took two quick steps and slammed my foot into the door, and then down the hall, from side to side, kicking each door and on down and around the corner and away.

"You can't do anything to change it. It's not you, or anybody else, it's me. Nothing about you is wrong."

"As coroner I'll vouch for her, she's not merely dead but really quite sincerely dead." Moto came in late, in a fine mood. "Let's short-sheet Rank." And Ford and I agreed. We stripped his bed, folded the top sheet in half and remade the covers, patted his pillow. And all there was left was the waiting. Moto pulled the little baby-casket cooler out from underneath his bunk and gave Ford and me a pop. "The reward of a thing well done," he said, raising his can, "is to have some Big Red afterward."

"Hitch your wagon to Big Red," Ford followed.

162

"More Big Red with less art," I said.

We got into bed, and Ford toed off the light, and we waited. Rank opened the door, paused for a moment, and then came the rest of the way in. We were all asleep, quivering. He took his clothes off, fumbled with his stereo and headset in the dark, and finally tried to get into bed. In my mind's eye I saw him, while I heard him, wrestling with the sheets, trying to jam his feet down into the bed and pull the covers up over his head. I held out as long as I could, but when Ford clicked on the flashlight and waved it at Rank, I let loose, howling and rolling in my bed, howling and rolling when Rank said, "What did you guys do?" howling and rolling till Ford got out of his bunk and clicked on the light again, to look up at me, to see if I was all right.

"Don't. Please, don't. Come on. Come here. Come on. I'm sorry."

Ford sighed, busted, "God, I can't stand this stuff," and let the cover fall closed from 90 degrees. I turned over in my bunk to get a better look at him. "How can you do well at something when you don't give a dog's ass about it?" All the lights were off but Ford's desk lamp. "I mean I just keep waiting for something to happen."

"It will," I said.

"I'm not coming back," he said.

"Sure you will."

"I ought to go home right now."

"What good would that do? What's back home?"

"That guy, I can't stand him." He pointed at Rank's bunk. "He's a true-to-life hypocrite."

"No, he's not. He believes every word he says."

"I don't believe that." He pushed his chair out from the desk and bent over to untie his sneakers. Then he raised back up and put his hands on his knees, looked up at me. "Why are you in bed so goddamn early?"

"No reason."

"I wouldn't ever say anything against her."

"I wouldn't want you to."

"Let's me and you go somewhere. Let's take the hearse and just go."

I didn't answer him. He undressed and climbed into his bunk. Moto and Rank still hadn't come in.

"Well," he said, "when the hell are you gonna stop sighing?" He said it to the ceiling.

"I don't."

"You do, all night long. Rank even said something about it. I almost punched him."

"I guess when you learn to roll over gradually in bed, instead of flipping like a shark's bitten you, like you can't stand your own goddamn life." I waited for him to say something back. I waited and waited, but nothing came and so I said, "Hey, I didn't mean that, you know. I was just kidding."

And he said, "I know. But I can stand it."

"Christ, yeah," I said.

"I just wish," he said, "I just wish I wouldn't get so frustrated."

"I'm sorry, I'm sorry."

I went down to the farm on a weekday, unexpected, and found Grandpa out in the side yard as I drove up, bundled in clothes and cap, as if he stood there at all times, waiting for someone to arrive. He leaned on the fender as I got out, and said, "Take a day off?"

And I didn't look at him but said, "Yeah."

And he started off toward the barn. He said, "Good boy."

I jammed my bare hands into my jacket pockets and followed him. I followed him through the barn and back to the garage while he asked yes-and-no questions and had me hand him things. We went in the house and back out and back to the cows and along the creek to see if it was frozen over yet and then back to the house where it was warm and we took off our jackets.

He said, "You make the tea."

And I did that, although I'd come to have it made for me. But he was just as nervous as I was.

"I don't want to say I don't love you. I'm just not enough in love."

No wind, no rain, and of light only that reflected, in my memory; and I myself knotted, thick, useless, narrow-eyed, and dumb, so that only her voice came through, her voice unbuffeted and saline, bodyless, like God's.

"I don't want it anymore. I don't want it anymore. I've changed."

21

W HAT DID he see? Me, here alone at my desk, telling the story over and over again, lifting the brick from my paper, hoping each telling time that the ending will be different? I do not doubt it. It is my comfort. He taught me how. He knew it works. I write and am written. The ending remains not the same.

What's to be said? I rub the callus on my finger and never know. The callus worn of rowing, paddling back and forth across Lethe, retrieving a memory at a time. It is slow work, but Zeke, my kind Cerberus, and I have all the time we need: It's exactly a life-long process.

I rub my callus and then sharpen the pencil to an idea's point to forestall the moment of beginning. Ah well, just begin, start with the last thing you said and go on from there. The beginning is not sacred. The end is very close to being sacred but at last it's not, only the whole of it matters, how you feel when it's over. Count on that. So I hold my hand just so and push off.

The page is deserted but dimpled, pock-marked, like the skin of a lemon, with indentations from the preceding page of pressure, winking implication that this page has really already been written and that I need only trace over the impressions there to get across. The thing to do is remember not to drown, and occasionally to lean out over the side for a drink. And although it is dark and there is no moon nor stars, there is a glare on the water and a lapping of waves upon the prow to steer by.

And the things brought back, so valuable that we entrust them to the safety of trees: paper and pencil, high shelves, stacked like cordwood against the winter. But the value is not only in the having, but in the bringing.

I lean back, rock back, and put my pencil down. What I cannot see, have, remember, I guess at, chop my memories to fragments and mix them together again, call it imagination. I don't know, and I keep asking myself why. There's a thread on the back of my shirt and I chase it the way Zeke would his tail. There is a coin taped to my knuckles but the rules allow me only the one same hand to retrieve it.

Why? An outright lie, faith shaken, a stab in the dark. Which of these? And who? Mary or me, my grandfather, his wife, Mother, Father, Us.

And the guessing provides no answer, nor the writing, but is the means of acceptance, is my way to say, "Well, okay," and more than that, to say I still love you all.

I pick up my pencil again and lean forward to write within the lines. I feel so powerful sometimes for all the things I have to remember. I scull back and forth, following the glare and the lap, the sight and the sound of it. I bring my memories back one at a time and place them all in a row.

The only orders I know are the time of day and that water finds its level. So time finds its level in each moment, and I am always swimming.

I finish a page and tear it from the pad and it rolls up like a scroll, like the word has become law, unreproachable, like a wave. But it isn't that; there's always the next page, this page, the last word. Things do not remain the same. And I am here to plead our faith in the species, to say that, at last, hope will not be lost. The story is not that I have hurt, but that I heal. The story is in the present tense.

I sit here and write, wanting more than anything else for my life to be memorable. And the writing, the process, becomes the proof. You can hold it in your hand.

22

"I'LL ALWAYS remember you."
And I said, "Fine."
"Hart."
"Please."
"Okay." And then a moment later, "I'm sorry."
"And that too, don't say that either."

All this in the half-dark of her dorm room, she sitting up on her bed, and me in the desk chair, swiveling back and forth a few inches at a time.

"This is just real hard," I said. "Look," I said, "for Christ's sake, Mary, don't let's do this." Her complacency, leaning against the dark wall, exasperated me. She was just letting something happen. "Goddammit, say something," I screamed at her.

"Say something, don't say something, what do you want?" She was screaming back at me, trying not to cry. "Don't ruin it, Hart."

"Don't ruin it? What was there? You care for me one day, you don't the next." I grabbed the back of the chair just to keep myself from railing back and forth in front of her.

"Don't ruin it. This isn't you."

"It's just not fair. It's like you're doing it all on purpose. It's like you picked me out of a line-up and said, 'I'll fuck him over.'"

"You wanted me too."

That sort of broke me. I let go of the chair and slumped back against the desk then. It was the way she said it in past tense. I sat there, trying to make out her face in the darkness, then folded in upon myself, jamming my gathered hands between my thighs. I said, "I still want you. If it's me, I can change. I really can. I just want to know what I've done. I can change with you. We can change together."

And then she said the thing that made me think she was a kid, that in her voice even sounded like it came from a kid, "But I don't want to," and I had no idea what to say to answer or call something like that, so I just sat there. Then she waited a moment before taking advantage of the silence, before she said, "I've got your stuff." She slid off the bed and pulled a box out from underneath it. My old sweater was on top, washed and folded. It sort of made me sick, the sight of it.

But I said, "Okay," and got up, and picked the box up, and walked some, and opened the door, and stopped, and said, "This is real hard," again, and she nodded, standing there across the room with her hand on her desk, and so I closed the door and walked some more, working on the walking.

168

And I broke out of the memory, woke up, and recognized my world. I woke, for the last month of the semester, the month without her, the last half of November, the first of December, deluged by thoughts and memories that were no different from the night's, the day's, the week's before. I woke up thinking, well, Mary will be along from The Pancake & Egg soon, and then remembering it wasn't so.

I stood under the shower closest to the open window and looked out through the steam. The sidewalks were deserted. Everybody who hadn't gone home was studying or asleep. I leaned out the window, the bar of soap in my hand. "Hey," I yelled. There is something about screaming "hey," even if there's no one to hear it.

I'd gone over her letters from the summer two or three times, looking for something, something to explain it, but it wasn't there. They read the same as they had before, always closed with love and longing, it seemed. The way mine had always closed.

I dried off and wandered back down the hall. Rank and Moto were up now, both studying. Ford still lay in bed. He rolled over when I came in.

"Any hot water left?" he asked.

"I think I was the first to take a shower."

I combed my hair and left it wet, and dressed. Moto was going over some equations for a physics final. Rank was rereading a chapter I knew he'd read a dozen times. He drove me crazy even when he was reading. I just didn't feel up to Chaucer at the moment, so I started out the door and downstairs for some cereal.

I passed Wyeth's room down the hall, and looked in. It was still dark. All the curtains were drawn to. Wyeth's roommates had all gone home. He was the only one left. He'd scheduled his classes so that all four of his finals fell on the last day of the test week. He was there, sprawled on his stomach in the middle of the floor, reading by the light of a little four-inch TV screen. "Scooby Doo" was on and he was reading *Great Expectations*.

"Wyeth?"

"Yeah? Yeah?"

"You okay?"

"Yeah. I'm almost finished."

His pupils were the size of quarters. "Why don't you turn on the light or open the curtains?"

"Morning is it?"

"It's late morning."

"Okay, okay."

And I left him there. I went downstairs and had my bowl of cereal. By the time I got back to the room Ford was back from the showers and Rank had his earphones on. He and Ford had stalemated. They rarely spoke to one another, and Moto had acted as a glass wall a couple of times, throwing himself in front of Ford when Rank got carried away.

I saw down and opened Chaucer's *Canterbury Tales*. Part of our final was based on a rote recall of the first eighteen lines of the "Prologue," and I hadn't even begun to memorize. I picked the book up and read through it once, then twice and three times, and each time I finished I couldn't remember a word of what I'd read. It just seemed totally useless. What was the use? I'd memorize it today, write it down tomorrow, and forget it the next day.

"When in April the sweet showers fall/And pierce the drought of March to the root," I said out loud, and everyone looked up at me.

"What's that?" Moto said.

Rank took off his earphones and the ant voices became a little louder. Ford grimaced.

I said, "When in April the sweet showers fall/And pierce the drought of March to the root."

And Moto said, "April is the cruelest month, breeding/Lilacs out of the dead land, mixing/Memory and desire, stirring/Dull roots with spring rain." Then he

170

paused, and asked, "You have to memorize something for English, don't you? I did that for my class. I knew some more but I forgot it."

While we were talking, Ford had reached over and clicked off Rank's stereo. Rank got up then, put away his book, and started to comb his hair. He couldn't take his shower because we were all in the room. We were usually gone to class by now.

"April. When in April the sweet showers fall/And pierce the drought of March to the root." Goddammit, this was insane. I stood up and paced through the room running the words over my lips. April April April. When in April. Hey. I hate myself for this. I could make love to you forever. Pierce the drought of March to the root. When in April. Christ.

And then Rank, what, oblivious to the world, incredulous I was, asked, "Hart, aren't you and Mary going to the airport today?"

And Ford said, "You asshole."

Moto looked up. I stopped in my pacing. Rank went on, "I thought they were going to the airport, I thought he was taking her. I thought they were back together."

I said, "Why'd you think that?"

"Well, I knew you talked to her about it and I've been praying, Hart, for it, for that."

"You asshole," Ford said. "He's been doing fine."

"Don't call me that. I can pray if I want to. It's my right." And then he turned back to me. "Hart, if you just trusted"—and he was lost for words for a moment, excited and afraid—"trusted, you know, if you and Mary got together and talked about God for a little bit, I know it would work out." And he wasn't even looking at me, but at the brush in his hands—". . . just get with her and bring it up and see how you both feel and if you both can find Christ, and you need to do that, find Christ, and it will be all right, you won't need to sigh any more and . . ."

171

And Ford was up before either Moto or I could get between them, and he had Rank up against a bunk, yelling and shaking him by the collar of his shirt. "You asshole. Why don't you just work on yourself and leave us alone? Why don't you ever once smile, goddammit? You're the most unhappy son of a bitch I've ever met. He wants Mary, not Christ." And by that time Moto and I were pulling them apart.

Rank was hyperventilating, red in the face, screaming back at Ford as best he could, "You're just a bully. You're nothing but a bully." And he pushed away from all of us and ran out of the room.

Ford ran his hands over his forehead and threw himself back into his desk chair. "That guy . . ." And he lost what he was going to say and threw his hands out, exasperated. "Bully," he said, "I ain't no bully."

Moto yelled, "You need to leave him alone." It was the first time I'd ever heard him raise his voice.

Ford just turned and looked out the window. I went back over to my desk and sat down, held on to the book. April. When in April. Mary. Please. Mary. And so I got up again, before the heat fell out of me, picked up the keys to the hearse.

"Where you going?" Moto yelled after me.

I didn't answer him. I ran down the hall and downstairs, past Rank in the foyer, and outside to the hearse. I was overcome by the uselessness of my situation. I drove with the idea of how different my situation was from everyone else's.

I stopped at a gas station and filled up, and tried to call Grandpa from the phone there. No answer. It rang and rang and rang. Goddammit, where was he? I'd never been so mad at him. I waited five minutes and called again, and when he still didn't answer I swore and ran back to the hearse, thinking I could get there before he ever answered the phone. I'd told him I'd come down that afternoon to help get the cows and calves down into

172

the first pasture, next to the barn. A big snow was expected the next day and he was afraid for them, wanted them close to the barn and hay, where he could go out and watch without tramping through much snow.

I pulled up into his driveway and got out of the car, leaving the engine running. He must not have heard me drive up because he wasn't outside. I opened the garage door and yelled for him, and then ran down to the barn. He wasn't there either. I ran back up to the house and swung the door open wide. "Grandpa!"

"What?" he yelled back, out of the kitchen.

It startled me, and I shut the door hard behind me and stepped into the kitchen. "Why didn't you answer the phone?"

He looked up from whatever he was doing. "What's wrong with you?"

Christ, I was frustrated with him. "Why didn't you answer the phone?"

"I've been out all morning. You're early. You ready to go to work?"

"No, I came down to tell you I can't."

"Hart, I've got to get them down here. It's going to snow big."

"Look, I can't. I tried to call you. I've got to go somewhere. Just wait till I get back."

"Where are you going?"

"I'm going to Colorado."

"Hart, that won't do you any good."

"Just wait to move the cattle till I get back."

"That'll be a week."

"No, it won't. I'll hurry. I'll be back in three or four days."

"I won't let those cattle stay back there."

"Goddammit, those cattle survived twenty million years without you. They can handle a little snow."

"Don't talk to me that way."

I caught my breath. It sort of scared me. We were both silent for a few moments. He was shaking more than I was.

173

"I want you to call Ford or Moto for me, and tell them I'll be back," I said quietly.

"You haven't told them?"

"No."

"Hart, they'll want to be going home."

"I'll be back, dammit. They'll get to go. It'll just be a few days."

He pushed his chair back. "I don't think you should go. Did she ask you to come?"

"No."

"This isn't a movie, Hart. You can't steal a future that's not yours."

"Grandpa, don't talk to me that way. I'm a grown person too." I was about to start crying, so I turned and went out the door, closing it solidly. I got back in the hearse and as I started to roll back down the driveway he came out and waved me back. I stopped and got out, yelled, "What?"

He came trudging down the slope, stepping gingerly over the creekstone. He stopped on the other side of the door and said, "Do you need any money? Here." And he reached over the door and put a roll of bills in my pocket.

"I'll be back soon. Wait for me," I said, and I got back in the hearse and left him standing in the driveway, there in his socks. And I did not think of him again till I returned.

And so the road opened out before me like the trough of a wave, calm and only to be followed, asking nothing. Its existence was enough reason. It led, I thought, to the cessation of my fury. I thought I'd feel better when it was passed, the miles driven. And the driving itself was a sort of balm, but only that, just pressure, really, more of a procrastination than anything else. A place to do time. The trough of a wave, the curl above.

And I discovered, driving, that my curl, the wave in me, was anger. I foamed at the whole world, and rolled on toiling with her betrayal, the evil of it, the outright licentiousness. Christ, it was unfair. I had loved her. I loved her. I'd done my part. I was going down out of the knobs and back through Lexington, to Louisville, over

174

the great basin, through the rain and snow, to tell her I hated her. To tell her I'd been done a wrong. I wanted to tell her: Please, don't ever do this to anyone else.

And I drove, comforted and boiling with my fury, as fast as the hearse would take me, waddling in the trough like a great boat with her long wheelbase, leaving a shallow wake in the winter-slick roads of rain and light snow. Beyond Louisville, through southern Indiana and Illinois, to the left of the St. Louis Arch and splitting Missouri, through Kansas, flatness like I'd never known, even in Texas, and finally into Colorado and Denver and up the grade to Boulder—thirteen hundred miles. I stopped twice along the way, pulled into road parks and climbed over the seat into the back of the hearse, and fell asleep easier than I had in a month, knowing I was on my way to her. The whole trip, stops and all, took twenty-seven hours.

I arrived in Boulder in the evening of the next day, December 14, exhausted but hyperactive. I used some of the money Grandpa gave me to check into a motel and clean up. I hadn't brought anything, so I had to go out and buy another shirt and a razor, a toothbrush and paste. And still, after the shower, I hadn't lost the anger and I was sick with it and nervousness, sitting there on that lousy motel bed, and I thought for the millionth time that I should just leave her to herself, thinking what a complete fool I was to come this far, that I should just go back home.

But I didn't. I bought a map, and looked up her street, and felt so strange, looking up the address of someone I loved. I folded the map back up and started to leave, but didn't know whether to take the things I'd bought at the drugstore with me or not. And I stood there at the door a moment too long with my indecision and it turned to disgust and anger too. I slammed the door behind me and left.

Her house wasn't hard to find. I knew the address by heart from the letters of the summer. The house was in a block of houses that bordered the University. It was strange to look at it. She'd described it to me but this didn't look like it at all. Smaller, somehow. I thought of

175

her growing up there, how much I wanted to know everything about that and her, and it struck me as horribly unfair that I never would. I parked the hearse across the street and got out. I did everything, shutting the car door, locking it, walking, with a slow, sure motion, so as not to make any mistakes. I was already becoming confused. I crossed the street and walked up her sidewalk. I kept reminding myself: Tell her. Tell her not to do this to anyone else. She has to know that. Tell her. Knocking on the door and no one coming and then seeing the bell and ringing that, my whole body ringing with it, and then the footsteps behind the door. And it opened.

And it was Mary. She said, "What are you doing here?" As if I hadn't come for her, done it for her, and so I couldn't look at her, and looked instead on beyond her, into the house, back into the kitchen, at a gray-headed woman, who turned and looked at me. Stopped in the washing of her dishes. It was evening. They've just eaten, I thought. And I looked back at Mary and said, "I'm sorry," and she softened a bit, and said, "Oh, Hart," and I leaned against a porch post, trying to steady myself when I said this, said it, as firmly as I could but still gnarled, saying, "Please, tell me again why."

23

I PUT A BRICK upon my exorcism and venture out again into that darkness. I let the screen door slam to, looking for Zeke, but he doesn't come until I yell twice. "Where have you been?" I say, as he puts his bony snout between my legs and then snaps his head up. I shove him away and say, "Christ, Zeke, don't do that."

Then he and I queue up against the night to go check on cows.

It's April. I've forgotten all my astronomy from college but still recognize a skyful of stars when I see one. The stars become brighter as we walk out from under the glow of the porch light and into the field. Man, it is dark. Before I get my night vision I nearly trip over a simple clod, imagining it a clump of baby rabbits. I've done it before. They scatter like a bubble bursting. And you don't want to take another step. You know the whole earth is covered with clumps of baby rabbits, like land mines. But my eyes soon widen with the hidden possibilities, and after a few minutes I can even make out that blackguard himself, that ebony sniffer, Zeke. He moves like a piece of darkness.

We are anything but alone. The fescue is full of sound, the screams, whispers, and massed laughs of the grass. Do they make this noise during the day? My eyes must crowd it out. A dog barks on the next farm over and Zeke stops and cocks his ears. "Come on," I say, warning him. Know your allegiance. He has taken of late to running with the hounds. Maybe it's just the spring. A bird chirps from a bush as we pass through the gate and then we hear an owl down among the trees of the creek.

We walk down the slope of the field, slowly now, squinting for cows. I know they are here, low boulders of flesh in the high grass. Still, the first base *moo* startles me out of my wits and I feel like an about-face and a run for my life. It even sends a shiver, like snapping a water hose, along Zeke's back. We stop and stare harder and find that we are deep among them. Here a shape, there a mass, and there a moving darkness, a silhouette pasted on the night. A few stumble up as we pass through them, fanatic ovationers among the rest of an unimpressed crowd, embarrassed boys at an adult passing through the living room. It's really a useless operation, checking cows at night. You can't get a good count. So we usually end up just asking around, walking the perimeter, seeing that

177

none of them are sleeping with barbed wire. And we finish our fence walking, without incident, at the top of the hill.

I say to Zeke, "I am not the least bit sleepy. How 'bout you?"

Decatur is a moon below the horizon. Only its glow will ever show. I sit down on the grass with my back against a big tree, part of the fence, and look out from me. Zeke groans to a halt at my side and crumples to the ground, his vast head resting on his front paws. Even in the darkness I can see his eyebrows rise as he wonders at me. How can I convince him that I am not a god? He would never believe me in his belief. To tell him that I have just now realized the grass is dew-soaked would simply make him laugh. And I realize, sitting here above my flock, scratching Zeke's constantly itching rump, that sometimes I wish I were they, him. I'm envious of the ability to believe. These are somehow blessed. Lord, it must be comfortable.

I pat Zeke and get back up, and we move back down the slope and through the gate, and down toward the porch light. As we get closer I hear, pure and shuddering, the bonging of Grandpa's clock on the mantel. The whole house can't even hold it in. It and the light beckon us home. We come under the influence of the porch light, like a hundred other moths, and have to squint our eyes for the harshness of it. Zeke wants to come in again, but I don't let him. "Act your species," I say, after checking his water and food. And then: "And you stay home. Don't run off." And we stare at one another for a moment, me and my dog in the yard under the porch light.

I yawn and scratch my head, wandering through the house turning off lights. And finally back to my bedroom, where I find another moth, blundered in through my window to my desk lamp. I shoo him away and turn it off too. I put my wet sneakers under the bed, throw my socks around the room, and let my jeans crumple to the floor. Then I move over to the light switch. But before turning it off I look back and check my path to the bed. I hit the switch and then step quickly to the bed and pile in before I forget the way. I draw the sheet and covers up under my chin and then stretch. Jesus, this is great.

A car moves by on the road below and the lights move quickly around my room. And I think, remember to wake up tomorrow, early. And I think some more, listening to Zeke nudge his bowl across the porch, thinking how grateful I am for the myth, the hope, and the possibility. Asia pregnant in her stall. But knowing that I don't know. That I don't believe.

And I think, lying here, that at last it's not contradictory, not at all, to be envious of those who believe, really believe, and at the same time, hope that it never happens to you.

24

GRANDPA DIED on December 23, 1978, a week after I came back from Colorado. He'd been out with the cows the day after I left for Colorado, came in that evening and had a mild heart attack, and didn't do anything about it. He woke up the next morning and called the hospital and they came for him, put him in a bed. And there he contracted pneumonia, and died. He died.

She, Mary, had given me something. She'd bowed her head while I held on to the porch post and said, "I'm sorry. I'm so sorry," and cried, leading me up to her room, past her mother, crying all the way, leading me by the hand. And there, in her room, with her dolls all arranged on a little girl's bed, and pictures from high school tacked to the walls, she told me she wasn't coming back, that she'd decided to go on to some other place where she'd have more to learn.

And I said, "But that's not why, right—us?"

And she said, "No, that's not why. Hart, I don't love you."

"Then why did you act like you did?"

"Because I wanted to love you."

So I went away with that, called it a why and reason enough, that she had tried to love me, and called it a why all the way back to Kentucky, till I went numb with it and the road and her absence.

And I should have stopped to sleep. But I didn't. And thirty miles outside of Decatur, in broad daylight, I woke up remembering only that I'd fallen asleep and that I shouldn't have, and the hearse was screaming down through a median and I tried to stop but it was too late and the hearse ripped into a guardrail tearing off the skin on one side and finally flipping the car around 180 degrees, slamming it into a concrete abutment. The hearse rocked a bit and then was still. I was down on the floor on the passenger side. There was some kind of high gutteral sound coming out of my mouth and I consciously had to think to stop it. I recognized it at the time as complete outrage. It took a couple more seconds to realize I'd had an accident. I crawled up out of the seat and opened the door on the passenger side. I stood up and ran my hands over my arms and legs and then over my head. The only thing I could find was a bump on my head. I walked around the hearse and saw it a complete loss and I wanted to cry, I was so sick and disgusted with myself, but I couldn't, it was all wadded up in my throat. Other cars were already stopped and a state trooper came soon and looked me over. He sent for a tow truck and told me to get my head checked. He said it like a joke.

And then back at the farm, sitting in the tow truck and pulling up into the side yard, seeing the strange car and then Mom running out of the house and Dad after her. I thought Grandpa had called them about me.

And of the five or six days of his life remaining I remember very little, only a few things we said when they let him take the tubes out of his throat, and the sight of him. Him, his face and forearms, his hands above the sheets, him weak and trying to smile at us all, me and Mom, Dad, Moto, and Ford—who'd flown home when they found I'd left for Colorado, and flown right back when they heard about Grandpa—us and a few of his old friends, smiling at us all weakly. He knew from the first that he was lost.

I remember distinctly the hours of his burial. The hours Dad and I and Moto and Ford dug his grave on the island shaped like a Christmas ornament, next to his wife's grave. Carrying the casket over the footbridge and along the deer path, lifting it above the briers. And sometimes you find you love your mom for more than the fact that she nursed you. She didn't let anyone say anything at the funeral. She was his daughter and I was her son, and Christ, I loved her up on that hill. We and his friends made muddy the little animal path up the knobside. We stood there for a while, Mom and Dad and I up close, Moto and Ford and the friends behind us, and farther back, Mary. She'd heard from Moto, I guess, and come.

And then two of his old friends, and Moto and Ford and I, buried him, in front of everybody, crying and sweating with it, the old men who'd known him so much longer than me that I marveled at them.

And most distinctly I remember what we said in the few minutes we were allowed to talk to each other during the last days. Him pulling the tube off his nose and holding it in his hand and saying, "I had no right to say that to you, about the stealing. When your grandmother went away I'd have given my soul, and yours, to get her back." And later, about Mary, telling me, promising me, "Some good one will yet come for you."

And all I could think about, say, in my numbness, before he left, was "Please, remember me.

"Please," I had said, "remember me."

25

EAVEN AND EARTH, must I remember? Step forward, Tin Man. The clock tolls its single throinging note. I keep the briers out of the graveyard and throw the windblown limbs over the hill.

Moto and I came back to school the next semester—though, for Moto, it was his last at UK. Ford drove us to the airport in January and we tried to get him to change his mind and go back with us. I told him I had enough money to buy him a ticket, and that we'd work everything out when we got back up there. He said no. He said he wasn't happy there. Moto and I didn't know what else to do. Ford watched us get on the plane with his hands in his pockets. I looked at Moto as we walked away from him, but Moto didn't look at me. Things just change.

I think, with Ford, it was the fury of his inability to change the way things were, to become interested, to find something to trust. He expected everything, knew it was out there, but couldn't seem to grasp it. He never went back to school. He did a couple of years in the Navy and is out now, living in Florida in a goddamned camper.

And Moto left UK after his sophomore year and enrolled in a school back home. He's graduated, married, and has a little girl. I am so happy for him I could scream every minute I think about it. He never expected anything, was always purely reacting to life, never anticipating it. Christ, I smile when I think about him.

And I am here, being introduced in Decatur as Gude Scatter's grandson, so I'll have a head start with anyone I'm meeting. And the time in between that time and this, the three and a half years, has been this day on the farm.

I just had the wind knocked out of me for a couple of years. I don't think I even thought about it all till I moved in here full-time.

I lie here, my toes toward the sky, and watch the lights revolve around me. And then suddenly, down on the road, an interminable braking and squall of tires. And silence. Zeke.

This, goddammit, is what I've had to work with, what I am given to carve these words out of. This abysmal bliss of emotion. He is all right. I run outside and call and he comes skulking up the long driveway and into the glow of the porch light. He knows that I know he's been out on the road. "What's the matter with you," I say, quivering, and hold open the screen door so he can go inside. "Get in here." The blank page is a myth. The paper comes instead black as Zeke. I just take a sharp tool and scrape away the excess, down to what's bearable. The problem is not what to put down, but what not to leave. What not to take with you.

Zeke comes into the bedroom and does that sweet slow adage and pirouette in front of the cold heater that he is famous for, and I get back in bed. "Go to sleep," I say, and look for the reflection of my love-strewn eyes in his.

I sweat in my bed and calm down, begin to feel again the power of my memory. Please don't mistake this, my story is a love story too. I remember Ford, his sure voice, singing in the shower with us; and Wyeth, coming in from a basketball game, sweating, grabbing a fistful of day-old popcorn from a bowl in our room and drying his underarm with it; and Mary coming down the hill after the funeral, crying, telling me she'd come and stay that semester if I needed her. I don't now know where she is. Lord, how are her ankles? And Moto, do you remember him at the table with Virginia, nodding? Rank and his prayers. And Grandpa, on his deathbed, whispering to me that during the war he shot over their heads. I love my dear grandfather.

But I think things are going to be all right. I am starting to feel, of all things, a little lonely. It feels real good. I've begun to walk out of the house with the radio blaring so I'll feel I'm leaving something, that I'll have a voice, a humming, to come back to. Love is strong as death. It's as if I'm as sure of my fate as Grandpa was, that some good one will yet come for me. That my future will be far more poignant than my past. Some good one. I feel like it might happen at any moment. Her mind overflowing with wondrous similes, her womb full of our beautiful children. I don't know. I think I have chosen, in my own awkward way, a life of hope. I have so much faith in I don't know what.